BURNING GREED

A gripping murder mystery, full of suspense

DIANE M DICKSON

Paperback published by The Book Folks

London, 2018

ISBN 978-1-7909-2612-1

www.thebookfolks.com

For Tonia,
thanks for your help.

Prologue

When the match hit the petrol, there was a sudden and shocking flare of heat. Soaked fabric caught fire immediately, flames licking and running over the creases and edges. A choking pall of stinking fumes billowed upwards and he pulled his sweatshirt over his chin, covering his mouth and nose. He wanted to flee but had to wait and make sure that the fire had taken a proper hold.

He backed away as far as possible, groping behind himself with an outstretched arm. The door handle felt warm under his palm and by now the conflagration was roaring. Smoke stung his eyes and they ran with tears. Still he waited, until the heap on the floor at the bottom of the stairs began to move. He gasped, drawing in a lungful of fire blighted air; he doubled over coughing and choking, desperate for a clean breath, but he had seen it move.

He would have to go back, walk through flames, back towards the roiling smoke. And then he acknowledged the truth. She hadn't moved, the body had. Heat had made the muscles flex, caused the limbs to reach and stretch. As the knowledge hit home he retched and bent, vomiting violently, clawing at his throat as it scorched. Finally, the other smell reached him, the roasting meat smell, and he was done. With a sound that was part scream, part moan he turned and dragged open the door. With a final horrified glance at the hell he had created, he lurched through the entrance, which was untouched yet by the flames and fumes. He staggered out to the bliss of fresh air in the deserted passage. He moved further into the darkness, coughing and crying and retching, but he mustn't vomit again, not out here, not where it could be found. He clamped a palm over his mouth, picked up the bag and, with his other hand against the wall for support, he struggled to the end of the back alley, around the corner and away.

Inside the warehouse the flames wreaked their havoc, running along the rivulets of petrol until they hit the tyres of the first car. Now the stink of burning rubber joined the stew of smells. Paint on the expensive bodywork began to bubble and peel. By the time the first vehicle exploded the alarm had already been raised and the scream of sirens split the evening. The body didn't twist and bend anymore, the hiss of fluids had ceased and all that was left of a life was the charred shape at the bottom of the collapsed staircase.

Chapter 1

Tanya didn't want to be where she was. Not because Iffley was not a good area, though it certainly wasn't. However, the restaurant had been recommended and it was handy for them all. No, it wasn't that. She stood outside, staring in through the window. Inside she could see Charlie Lambert and his wife had already arrived. Carol looked well, she was laughing at something one of them had said. This was a good sign, surely. She had been fighting post-natal depression ever since Joshua had arrived. Charlie had told Tanya that when the approval for his transfer had come through, the chance of a move away, nearer to her sister, and the thought of a new start seemed to have helped. "We're not out of the woods yet," he'd said, "but it's looking good."

The couple were sitting at the long table in the corner with Kate Lewis and the youngest member of what had been her small team, Dan Price. Not for the first time Tanya felt a bit sorry for the young women who would lust in vain after the detective constable. Shy and awkward he was, in spite of his six feet in height and his good looks. She liked him. She had come to like all of them as they had worked together, even Paul Harris who could be a bit coarse, very un-PC. The only one she really had a problem with was Sue Rollinson. The detective constable's loyalty to Charlie was verging on hero worship, possibly infatuation, and had been the cause of friction. Tanya shrugged, it didn't matter now. The team was almost certainly going to be broken up and reassigned.

When he told her that he was applying for a relocation, away from Oxfordshire, Tanya had smiled and nodded and uttered encouraging words, but what she really wanted to say had been, "Don't go, Charlie. You're the nearest thing I've had to a mate in years."

She'd had no choice but to bite back the words. He was ambitious, and she recognised the drive, the greed for success; she had it in spades herself. She was driven by the need to do well and if he believed, as he obviously did, that his progression towards one of the top jobs in the police force meant that he had to move away, then that was his right, and his choice. She was going to miss him. He'd saved her life not all that long ago and before that, when they first met, when she was drafted in to take over his case, he'd been dignified and professional. He could have been difficult and obstructive. There weren't many people like him that you came across and now he was going to be in Liverpool. Okay, it was only a bit more than a hundred miles away, but he would be part of another force, effectively out of her life.

She altered her focus a bit, saw her own reflection in the glass. She flicked her glance up and down. Her new dress had been expensive, but quality showed in the way it clung to her figure, and the new boots were gorgeous. She knew it was shallow, but new stuff cheered her up. She painted a smile on her face and pushed through into the restaurant, waving to the others as she came nearer to the table.

"No sign of Sue and Paul yet?" she asked.

Charlie had stood to kiss her cheek, a familiarity allowable now outside of work.

"No, they're sharing a taxi and there's some sort of hold up in town. A fire, I think," he said.

"Oh right, I heard the sirens as I was driving in. Well, we might as well get a round in while we wait, eh?" As she spoke she waved to the waitress.

"I'll get these," Charlie said.

"No, it's on me." She let her smile cover them all. "This is probably the last time we're together, so I reckon it's my shout."

He didn't put up much of a fight and they all knew that, as senior investigation officer on their last job, it was pretty much expected of her.

They ordered drinks and chatted for a while; they didn't talk about the last case. It was done, a reasonably successful outcome, although two dead victims would have a place in Tanya's memory for a long time, probably always. Tonight though, Charlie was centre stage telling them about the new job as a detective inspector with the Merseyside force, his impressions of the city and the rented house they'd be using until things were settled.

Tanya glanced at her watch, it was almost half past eight and they had been waiting for an hour with still no sign of the other two. She pulled out her phone and dialled Paul's number.

"Paul Harris." The phone was answered quickly.

"Hello, any idea how long you're going to be? We're starving to death here."

"Sorry, boss, it's pretty bloody messy out here, to be honest. I don't think it's a huge fire from what I can see but there are plenty of appliances and the roads are shut all over. I had a quick word with one of the fire officers, a mate of mine, it's a small warehouse that's involved. The main worry apparently is it spreading to other buildings. Anyway, top and bottom of it is we'll be about ten minutes now, according to Shamar, our driver."

"I'll get your drinks in ready, what are you having?"

She relayed the information to the rest of the group, bought another round of drinks and for a while they searched the internet on their phones to see what information there was about the cause of the delay.

There wasn't much. Not yet.

Chapter 2

With a glass of wine half-drunk, Tanya felt herself relaxing. She began to enjoy the banter and chat. Charlie was going, and she hated that, but for now she pushed it aside.

It was almost midnight before they finished eating, the late start had delayed things anyway, and then they had gone the whole hog with starters, desserts and coffee. Tanya had her phone on vibrate and once or twice as it jiggled in her bag, she had glanced down at the screen to see her sister's emoticon leering at her.

Fiona, up in Scotland with her perfect children and her perfect husband and her charity work. It wasn't that they argued, it wasn't really that she disliked her only living blood relative – they just had nothing in common. The slights and unfairness of a childhood where she had been forced into second place by her sibling's brilliance still hurt, and they had quite simply drifted apart. Nowadays there were greeting cards and the odd weekend when it was a milestone birthday. It was enough. When the phone buzzed a third time she began to wrack her brains, trying to remember what she had forgotten. Nothing came to mind. She would call her tomorrow, apologise for whatever it was.

The fourth call was as they were winding up to leave. It was the despatcher, she pulled the handset out of her bag and mouthed a 'sorry, work' at the others as she stood and moved away from the table.

Tanya handed her credit card to the cashier and, still speaking into the phone, she turned to look back at the table. She wanted Charlie, but it was out of the question, *Sod it, why not.* She caught Sue's eye and waved a hand to call her over.

The other woman arrived just as the cashier handed the card back. Tanya reached for it. He leaned close, spoke quietly, "I'm sorry, Madam, that card has been rejected."

"What? Are you sure?" She turned the piece of plastic in her hand as she spoke.

Sue was already fishing in her bag, a smug grin on her face, "It's okay, boss, I've got this."

"No, no that's not what I wanted. It's a mistake. Oh, look." Tanya slid another card out of her wallet and handed it across the counter. "I haven't got time to argue, use this one."

While the payment was processed, Tanya leaned close to the other woman. "I need you to come with me. That was control. We have to go down to the fire site."

"What now?" Sue asked.

"Yes, are you sober enough?"

"Yeah, of course. What's happened?"

"There was a body in the building. Thing is though, the preliminaries indicate that an accelerant was used. It's looking dodgy. We're going down to have a look, speak to the fire officer and what have you. Can you go back, alert the others and tell them I'll call them in the morning early if it looks like there's a job on?"

"What about Charlie?"

"Well, what about him?" The payment had been accepted and Tanya was juggling with her coat, bag and wallet; she shook her head, frowning.

"Well, is he in?"

"I shouldn't think so. After all, he's not really one of us anymore, is he?" It hurt as she said it, much more than she had expected it to.

As Sue took the message back to the table, Tanya contacted the station to ask them to send a car. She could have called a taxi but a blue and white would get them there quicker. As she pushed the phone back into her bag a text alert chimed, Fiona again.

Chapter 3

The whole area was filthy. Pools of oily water lay on the ground, blue lights reflecting on wet, dark walls. The air was thick with fumes and soot. "Shit," Tanya rubbed at black flecks on her sleeve, smearing them across the fabric. She glanced at her boots, the pale leather was darkened with water and they were splashed with mud and grime. She glanced at Sue, beside her. Her plain Doc Martens, black trousers and top weren't showing any of the filth that must be there. She seemed unaware of the soot falling onto her head and shoulders. Tanya clamped her mouth shut, resisted the temptation to pull out a handkerchief and rub at her feet. The boots were ruined anyway, and she wasn't giving the other woman any reason to sneer behind her back.

Sue for her part was pulling her long black hair away from her face and screwing it into a sleek bun with a little glittery scrunchy. Tanya peered through the darkness trying to find someone who looked as though they might be in charge. When they had shown their warrant cards to the uniformed constable positioned at the end of the alley, all he'd been able to tell them was that the bronze commander had gone inside the building with the medical examiner a while ago, but he wasn't sure where they were now.

Tanya grabbed the arm of a passing firefighter, the woman turned and shrugged off the hand. "Press people, back beyond the tape." In response Tanya lifted her ID nearer to the woman's red-rimmed eyes.

"Sorry, police," she said, "I need to speak to whoever is in charge right now."

"Oh right, my mistake." The firefighter grinned, her teeth stark white against her smoke-blackened face. "You looked a bit dolled up to be official."

"We came straight from the pub." As she answered, Tanya's irritation grew. She didn't need to justify her appearance, but the comment had made her feel ridiculous. Sue had taken a couple of steps away, towards the smouldering building. "Anyway, any idea where I can speak to whoever is in charge?"

Jerking her thumb in the direction of a small huddle of people, the firefighter stomped away, shouting out to her colleagues to 'hang on a minute'.

As they walked across the roadway, stepping over hoses and around piles of dark and smoking detritus, she spotted Simon Hewitt, the medical examiner. He turned and raised a hand in recognition. Tanya smiled back at him and nodded. He stepped aside, making room for the two women to join the small group. Simon introduced Tanya to the bronze commander.

"So, what can you tell me?" she asked.

"Not a lot at the moment. Your colleague here, Dr Hewitt, has been in and had a look; so he can tell you more about the victim than I, though even then, don't expect much." He glanced at the medical examiner who shook his head. "As far as the incident goes, the dogs have alerted that there was an accelerant used. It's still very early days and we are just finishing off and damping down. It wasn't a huge fire as these things go but there is extensive damage to the interior, and of course, sadly, there has been a fatality. More than that I can't say right now."

"Can we go inside, have a look?" Tanya asked.

"I'd prefer if you didn't just yet. Paul, here," he indicated the cameraman, "has got some video and some stills, there will be footage from the personal cameras as well, but really, it's not safe yet. I don't want civilians in there."

"I wouldn't class us as civilians, Officer Bartlett."

He gave her a small smile, "Well, I'm sorry, Detective Inspector, but I would. It's for your own safety."

Tanya had no choice but acquiesce, but she hadn't missed the smirk that had crossed Sue Rollinson's face. Had she made a mistake bringing her instead of one of the blokes, or Kate? *Ah well too late now.*

"So, when will I be able to have access?" she asked.

"Tomorrow, probably late morning, maybe later depending on the extent of the damage. The mezzanine level will be unsafe for longer and may have to be demolished. I can have someone call you." He held out a hand and Tanya passed over one of her business cards.

"Thanks." She turned to Simon Hewitt. "Doesn't seem a lot of point hanging around now. Will you let me know before you come and take the body? I'd like to see it in situ."

"Of course. I'll have Moira call you." They smiled at each other, acknowledging the ongoing tension between Tanya and the snarky receptionist who ran the morgue with a rod of iron.

"Thanks for that!" She turned and walked away, knowing that Sue would have no choice but to follow and counted it a small, if petty, victory when she heard the dull thud of the Doc Martens splashing through the puddles to catch up.

Once they were away from the worst of the muck and out of the way of the fire brigade, Tanya said, "Right, Sue, I'll have to speak to the DCI but I don't think we can start much just now. I'm going to assume that we'll be assigned. Can you call the others and let them know? Ask them to report in the morning, eight o clock will be early enough under the circumstances."

She stopped and pointed high up on the corner of the wall. "CCTV. First thing I want you to get on to that. We need to see who's been in and out of here. Get me copies. Right, can you get yourself home okay?"

As she turned and stalked back towards the waiting squad car, she dialled the number for Bob Scunthorpe, the detective chief inspector, to bring him up to date and confirm that it seemed that there was a case to investigate. She knew that she had probably caused herself a problem leaving Sue to get a cab, but the smirk on her face in front of the bronze commander had rankled. She felt just a bit smug as the driver opened the car door and she slid into the rear seat.

Chapter 4

Tanya was awake early making notes, planning her first actions. There were calls to make, and at seven-thirty, which she judged late enough, she called Bob Scunthorpe. She was keen to have him confirm first off that it would be her case. The DCI was being driven to his office and had nothing more than she had told him the previous evening.

"Have you anything new?" he asked.

"Not as yet. Dr Hewitt was there last night, I am going back with him today as soon as the fire service tell us it's safe. They contacted the key holder last night on his mobile. Name of Alan Parker. He's away. Dubai. At a car show apparently, but is heading back soonest. The secondary keyholder is his wife, Julie. She was away also, visiting her mother in Cornwall. She is going to be available this afternoon."

"No idea who the victim is?"

"Not as yet, sir."

"Okay, come in and see me in an hour. I think your team is still available."

"Yes, sir, great." This would have been a chance to change things, but it was already too late. After last night, given the obvious problem that still lurked between them, she wanted Sue removed but then, how could she explain why she had taken her to the scene? She couldn't explain it to herself, it would have been so much more logical to have taken Kate, who had seniority, or Dan. Why Sue? Was she trying to impress the woman? No, stupid thought. Was she trying to win her over, and if so why? She had never been bothered about making friends before. Maybe this was just some odd disquiet, a leftover from their first encounter, and now she was stuck with it. Well, they'd just have to be grown up about it, wouldn't they?

With an exception for the Control's number and Bob Scunthorpe's, her phone had been in 'do not disturb mode'. It had seemed logical. She'd wanted a good night, wanted to start the day bright and ready to go. She hadn't been alerted to the texts coming in from Scotland. One after the other – *Call me. Call me please, urgently, it doesn't matter what time. Where are you, please call me.* And then the final one at just after four in the morning. *Tanya, For God's sake call me, Serena is missing.*

Serena. Which one was Serena? The oldest girl, was that Serena? She glanced at the framed picture on the wall in the hallway. Yes, and then Janet the younger girl and little Danni – Danielle – although she must be more than ten now. There had been nothing since the text at four, nearly five hours ago. Probably the girl had turned up, some teenaged tantrum that her sister had overreacted to. The phone had been on for a while now and there had been no calls. She would ring later. Fiona would be steaming, she didn't like to be ignored. There would be a long tense conversation and all the past imagined slights would be paraded. There wasn't time for that now, there was important work to do. Anyway, if the family had been up until four o'clock waiting for the girl to come home they'd still be in bed.

Chapter 5

Bob Scunthorpe offered her coffee and for once Tanya accepted. She had meant to call at Costa on the way in, but there were still detours around the fire site, and she had needed to be at work.

Bob picked up his mug and leaned back into the big, black desk chair. He nodded and waited for Tanya to take the lead.

"We don't have any more than last night, sir. Once I have the incident room set up, I'll get back in touch with the fire service's bronze commander, to see if I can hurry things up a bit. I'm seeing Mrs Parker this afternoon, she confirmed by text that she'll be available after lunchtime. Her husband has told her that he will be in tonight. They are not aware that there is a victim as yet. I wanted to tell her myself, gauge her reaction for one thing and of course, if there is a chance that it *is* a family member, we need to be sensitive. There are no children, but it could be a staff member or another relative. I am hoping that I'll have more information from Dr Hewitt, gender at least, before I speak to her. Apart from that, it's a bit of a hiatus right now. I'm waiting for CCTV from the entrance, I'm hopeful that will give us something concrete to work with."

"Plenty for you to be getting on with, setting up and so on," Scunthorpe replied.

"Oh yes, sir." Tanya took the hint, gulped back the last of her coffee and left.

The incident room was the same one they had used before. Tanya opened the door just long enough to glance round and say good morning. The team had automatically claimed the same desks and set the room up in the way that was familiar. On the whiteboard was the name Locksmith, the operational name generated by the computer. There were already a few images, the fire-blackened interior of the building and the twisted shape lying in filthy water which could only be the corpse. Kate was in organisation mode, labelling the pictures.

Tanya strode past, on the way to her own office to take a minute to look at personal messages and listen to her voicemail. Charlie was sitting behind the bigger desk, the one he had been using since they had first shared the space. He looked up as she spoke.

"Oh, it's you," she said.

"Hiya, Tanya. I'll move. You'll be using this one, yeah? I came in to finish some last-minute paperwork, grab some of my bits." Charlie pointed to the cardboard box on the chair, his framed family pictures and pen pot in the bottom.

"You're okay, Charlie. I didn't expect to see you, that's all. You carry on, really, I'm going through…" She waved a hand in the direction of the other room and the activity. He nodded. He seemed embarrassed.

"I'll see you later, maybe? Coffee perhaps?" she asked.

"Great. Listen, do you mind if I…" He jerked his head in the direction of the incident room. "I'm not going up to Liverpool until the end of next week now, bit of a delay their end – something administrative. I'm going to be hanging around like a spare part."

"You could go home." As she spoke she realised how unfriendly it sounded. "Well, what I mean is, you must have plenty to do, with the house move and all."

He lowered his head, nodding, his mouth turned down.

She took a breath, "No, actually why don't you come in? If you're going to be here anyway."

He looked up and grinned. "Right, good. Carol's already up at her sister's and the house is half packed. She went up this morning and it's a bit grim and quiet, you know."

"Well, come on, sit in. It's all good." They walked down the corridor together. Though it was fun to see the surprise on the faces of the others when they walked into the room together she couldn't decide how she really felt, having him there, but not part of it. Sue's eyes had widened as she grinned at Charlie.

"Okay, Charlie's hanging about like a spare part so he's sitting in for a day or so, unofficially. Let's get on with things."

Finding him there, in the office, had thrown her and she'd forgotten to log on to her personal email account. When she opened her laptop and booted it up, she was hit with multiple messages from her sister, the last one just half an hour ago. She didn't have time now, but that was something she'd have to deal with.

It didn't take long to share the small amount of information with the team, and then the call came from Moira at the morgue. Taking Sue, because it seemed logical after the night before, and she was being 'adult' about it, they left for the scene of the fire.

In the car, Sue was quiet, no mention was made of the abandonment of yesterday and the silence felt loaded and awkward. Tanya was irritated. This was something that she was going to have to deal with or the junior officer would have to go. She knew that to do that would put a black mark on her record though, and as a woman, she felt a degree of loyalty to others of her gender. Still, it wasn't enough to be a woman, you had to shine, you had to stand above the rest and Sue wasn't doing that. In fact, she was behaving like a spoiled kid, still holding a grudge; and it wasn't even her own grudge, it was on behalf of Charlie. It was time to move on.

"Chase up the CCTV footage, we need that as quickly as possible and we need to talk, Sue. Come and see me later, before you go home," Tanya said.

"Okay."

"Okay *ma'am*, okay *boss*. Either is fine."

"Yes, ma'am," Sue muttered as she turned her face to stare out of the window.

Tanya's sighed, she really didn't have time for this.

Chapter 6

There was still a fire appliance parked at the end of the short alleyway. There were no hoses and the crew were tidying up around the site, no sign of urgency now, just routine. A small red van was nearer to the warehouse and as Tanya and Sue picked their way across, Chief Fire Officer Bartlett emerged, stretching up to his full height and putting on his uniform hat. He held out his hand to Tanya, nodded at Sue.

"Dr Hewitt is inside already," he said. "We have some protective gear for you."

Tanya held up the blue bundle of her forensic suit.

He nodded. "You'll need more than that."

They walked to the van where a young firefighter issued them with hard hats, to go over the hoods of the all-in-one suits, and they grinned at each other – a moment of lightness.

"Firefighter Morley will take you in. Stick close to the route she shows you and don't lean on anything. Do not make any attempt to access the upper areas and keep away from the staircase. We are still making safe. If you need anything more from me just let me know." With a brief smile he turned and marched back down the alley to his waiting car, his courtesy at an end. Before he had disappeared, they were being ushered forward into the warehouse.

The smell was chemical, acrid and harsh. As they reached the bottom of what had been a staircase but was now a blackened and broken skeleton of one, Simon Hewitt stood from his crouched position. He rubbed at his back, stretched his arms above his head and rotated his shoulders.

"Detective Inspector, good to see you. Shame it always has to be under these sorts of circumstances. We should do something about that."

Tanya was peering down at the ghastly vision on the ground. Teeth grinned obscenely from a grimacing, lipless mouth and the rest of the body was shrunken, the arms reaching upwards, knees drawn towards the torso. She knew she could never unsee this, and the only thing to do – for it to sit more easily in her mind – was to find out why and how someone had been reduced to this dreadful thing, barely recognisable as a human.

"What can you tell me?" She had knelt on the filthy floor and she turned to peer up at Dr Hewitt.

"From the size of the body, I think what we have here is a female, or possibly a slight male, maybe a teenager. The charring is extensive, and I would suggest from my own preliminary examination, and from conferring with the fire investigator, that this poor woman, probably a woman, was already laid here when the fire started. As you can see, although we haven't turned it yet, the body is burned much more extensively on the front. He had crouched beside Tanya and indicated what they could see of the back where the skin wasn't so black and burned. I think that when we move her, we may find less damaged tissue and that will give us a chance for DNA. No fingerprints obviously, but we will have the teeth and jaw to work with for dental records."

Tanya looked at the victim. "Laid down?"

"Yes, I think – and again this is very early, almost speculation to be honest – that she was already on her back, then the accelerant, which was most likely petrol, was poured onto her and set alight."

"So, she may have already been dead when the fire started?"

"Oh, I sincerely hope so, Inspector; or at least unconscious. I'll let you have my report as soon as I've had a chance to have a look at her in the morgue." He called out to a couple of suited figures who had been standing to one side, labelling evidence jars and placing them carefully into boxes. "If you could help me, gentlemen?"

Tanya didn't want to watch. She stood and walked to another group who were photographing the vehicles. She held out her hand to the senior investigator and introduced herself and Sue. "What have we got here?" she asked.

"Well, as you can probably tell, we've got two cars. I think they'll need a bit of a touch up to the paintwork." The photographer gave a sharp laugh. Tanya forced a smile. Although her mouth was hidden by the mask she knew that her face would lift, her eyes crease and they would tell she was joining in with the fun and games. She didn't want this, but it was the way people coped. Gallows humour to get them through the horrors. It had never worked for her, but she heard Sue give a little giggle beside her. She tipped her head to one side, raised her eyebrows, and waited for further information.

"I think we have identified that one." The man pointed with a gloved finger to a low car, the red paint blistered and stained, tyres burned away, but recognisable. "Probably a Ferrari, we'll have to wait until we have the VIN to know exactly. And this other..." He turned and nodded at the heap of charred fabric and twisted metal. "Well, not sure, but it's not a minibus." Again, the hollow laughter.

"So, a Ferrari, that's pretty special, isn't it?" Tanya said.

"I'd say so, yes. The other one is much more badly damaged, but I reckon it's a sporty Honda. What do you think, Dave?" he said, addressing his colleague.

"Yeah, Honda almost certainly."

Tanya blew out a breath, nodded. "Okay, thanks. How soon will we be able to get up there?" She pointed towards what was obviously an office on a mezzanine floor, suspended and unreachable above the remains of the staircase. The safety rail was all but gone, but the walls were still standing. However, the underside of the floor was blistered and warped by the heat.

"Oh, that'll be a while, you can see the danger. I'll make sure they let you know, could be it'll never be safe enough for you to go up."

"Thanks." Tanya turned to go, and as she stepped away, she twisted back. "Oh, just one more thing, who called it in, do you know? Who reported the fire?"

"Hold on." Tony Lyle clicked on his tablet. "Hmm, a member of the public smelled the smoke. I'll send the details on, shall I?"

"Yes, please, I'll leave a card with someone outside." Tanya nodded and then, with their suits rustling and feet splashing through the pools of water, they made their way out into the relatively fresh air of the narrow alleyway.

Chapter 7

Back in the car, Tanya made a few notes on her tablet before driving out towards the main road.

"So, you going to take him up on it, boss?" Sue sounded friendly.

Tanya glanced across the car, frowning. "Sorry?"

"Dr Hewitt," Sue said, "meeting him away from dead bodies and stuff?"

"I haven't a clue what you mean."

"Right, okay. Sorry." Sue turned back to the window, the attempt at conversation over, her shoulders hunched slightly away. Tanya shook her head and drove on.

The mobile phone had connected automatically to the in-car audio system, so when the tweet came from her sister, Tanya was left with little choice but to listen to it, read out in the robotic voice of the device.

'Christ Tanya ring me.' It said, *'I have been trying to reach you for hours we are out of our minds here. Ring me.'* The call ended with the question from the phone, *'Do you wish to send a message?'*

Sue, turned, her eyes wide. "Hmm, somebody sounds upset." There was a short pause before she added, "Boss."

"Oh hell. Yes, it's my sister. Apparently, her daughter has gone missing. I should have got back to her, but I haven't had the chance and I thought that by now it was all okay."

"How old is she?"

"My sister, she's older than me by seven years."

"No, the kid. How old is the kid who's missing?"

"Oh Serena, erm… I'm not sure. Maybe she's about sixteen?"

Sue, from a large, Indian family was staring across the small space a look of disbelief on her face. "You don't know how old she is, your own niece?"

"Well no, not exactly, we don't keep in touch that much, to be honest."

"Are you not worried? Haven't you done anything?"

"Fiona fusses a lot. She thinks the world revolves around her; well, in fairness, it used to − pretty much." Tanya paused, she didn't share this stuff, her past, and for certain Sue wasn't the one to open up to. "Look, I just thought it would all be okay, but it seems not, yet. I'll have to get back to her, obviously. We're here now. You go in and bring them up to date. Ask Kate to confirm my appointment with Mrs Parker at…" She glanced at her watch. "Two. Give me a few minutes to deal with this."

"Of course. Hey, listen, if I can do anything else, let me know, I'm really sorry about this. This is awful." In the face of what she hoped was over re-action on Sue's part, Tanya felt a nudge of unease. Surely this was just some sort of minor thing, it would all be over in no time.

She'd worked in missing persons. Missing kids, it happened over and over and then they turned up again when they'd got the sulk out of their system. But not always. She knew that better than anyone. Sometimes the ending was ghastly and heart-breaking and sometimes, far too often, there wasn't an ending and families waited for years, always wondering if today would be the day that they found out what had happened, and why, and whose fault it all was.

She had a flash in her mind of the dreadful burned body they had just left. Somewhere, there must be someone thinking that woman was missing, maybe they were ringing around friends and relatives. Her throat constricted and she felt moisture on her palms where they gripped the wheel. She couldn't remember Serena very much, but surely nothing could have happened to her, not to her sister's child.

Chapter 8

Sue turned from the corridor into the incident room. Tanya raised a hand in greeting to the rest of them but hurried on past. In her own space she dropped her jacket and bag on the visitor's chair. Charlie wasn't there, and she breathed a sigh of relief as she took out her personal mobile to call Scotland.

"Tan, at last. I've been trying for hours, where the hell have you been?" Fiona sounded angry, but that had been expected, it was more than that though, there was a note in her voice that Tanya had never heard before. Her cool, 'together' sister sounded on the edge of panic. Tanya's throat dried in response to the hint of hysteria.

"I'm sorry. It was work stuff. There's been an incident and I just haven't had a minute." It wasn't true, she could have, should have, made time, but she had simply not wanted to deal with this, with family stuff. She hadn't wanted any part of a soap opera with her sister's kids. She could tell though, that she had made an error of judgement. She didn't compound it by asking the obvious but pointless question. There was no way Serena had come home.

"Look, I'm sorry, okay. Just tell me what's happening. You've called the police – yes?"

"Well, of course I have. I called them yesterday, much good it did me. They just told me to wait, to give it time. They didn't even come to see us for hours."

"Okay, well they would just be following protocol, never mind about that. What is the situation right now?"

"They've taken some details. They sent a bloody kid to speak to us, a woman, well nothing more than a girl really. She made some notes and said they'd get back to us. They haven't. You need to come. You need to sort this out. You worked in missing persons. You've got to come and sort this. Tanya, you have to get her back."

"Fiona. You really need to calm down."

"Calm down! Have you not heard what I've said? Serena is missing. I haven't seen her since yesterday morning. I have no idea where she is, and nobody is listening to me."

"Yes, I see. I know it's upsetting, it's scary, but we have ways to deal with this, ways that work. I'm sure they have listened. Now, when you last saw her, what was the situation then? Had you had a row?"

And so it began, the question and answer session that she had been through so often before and never thought to be doing with her own family. Tanya found that she slipped easily into the routine, gathering the information, sorting what was important from what the girl's parents thought mattered. Trying to work through the defensiveness of responses geared to hide family friction. Sorting truth from confusion.

The girl had left for college as usual. After the response from Sue Rollinson, Tanya was prepared for the horrified reaction when she had to ask exactly how old her niece was, where she went to college, what she was studying. She didn't bother with apologies, it was what it was, and outrage wasn't going to help. In response to the repeated demands for her to travel immediately to Scotland, she reacted as coolly as she could. Of course Fiona thought she should be there. She obviously believed that Tanya could simply waltz into another force's offices and start dishing out orders, pulling rank, demanding special attention. It was what her elder sister would have done, and it was almost impossible to convince her that the police service didn't work that way. Not at her level anyway. She wasn't a Mason, obviously. She didn't have high flying contacts, and even if she did they wouldn't be able to do any more than the local force's missing persons section were, undoubtedly, already doing.

The longer they talked the more unreasonable Fiona became and when, to Tanya's disbelief, verging on horror, she began to beg and to cry Tanya knew that it was time to cut the call and try to do something that might be worthwhile.

"I'll give them a call, Fiona. I'll find out what's happening and get back to you."

"So, you're not coming up here then. You're not going to come even though your own niece is missing?"

"No, I can't. I have just started a murder inquiry. There's no way I can leave right now."

"I see, so some dead stranger is more important than your own family?"

"No, that's not it at all. I'll see what I can do to help, but from what you've told me, she took clothes with her, she was at college as normal and she has taken money from her bank account. It sounds as though she has gone of her own volition. I know that doesn't help you, but it does change the way that we look at things. She didn't take her phone and that's odd with a teenager, so she obviously doesn't want you to be able to contact her. It doesn't sound, well…" Tanya hesitated. "It doesn't sound as though she has been taken by force." Though she believed it as she said it, she sent up a silent prayer to a God she wasn't sure she really believed in, that what she was saying was true.

Her sister's voice was cool now, ice through the ether, "I would have thought that you, of all people, would know about grooming, about filthy old men luring away young girls. I would have thought that you would have taken this seriously. But no. I know we had problems in the past, Tanya. I know you have always felt jealous of me, thought I was favoured more than you."

Tanya didn't answer, she knew that had been the case for all her childhood and teenage years and what was more, she knew that Fiona was fully aware of the different treatment they had received. She had been the special, talented and gifted elder daughter and Tanya the also-ran. The inconvenient mistake, born when her parents thought they had finished with babies and were concentrating all their efforts on ensuring that Fiona had the best that they could possibly give her from their modest means.

She had clenched her fist so hard that, when she uncurled her hand later, there were red half-moons dug into the palms. Now though, she would not enter into a slanging match with her panicked, grieving sister. "I'll do what I can. Fiona. I'll get back to you very soon."

"You've let me down. I know you don't think much of family, but you have let me down." And with that, the conversation was over. Tanya clicked off her phone and lowered her head into her hands. She didn't need this extra pressure, not right at the crucial start of what was almost certainly a murder inquiry. She didn't hear Charlie come in and, until he spoke, hadn't realised she was not alone.

"You okay?" he said quietly.

She jumped, sat up blinking at him, stared for a moment before she spoke, "No, not really, Charlie." And she told him about Serena.

Chapter 9

Charlie hadn't had time to react, except for the monosyllables of sympathy as he listened, when Kate Lewis knocked and pushed open the office door.

"Sorry to interrupt. You've got that appointment, boss, with Mrs Parker, and if you don't leave soon you'll not make it. She lives the other side of Oxford and if the traffic's bad you'll be late."

"Right," Tanya said, "yes, I hadn't forgotten, thanks, Kate. Can you ask Sue to get ready to come with me? Will you take over the CCTV reviewing? It's going to be staring at a dark wall mostly but if there was anyone around we need to speak to them as soon as possible. I'll be out in a minute."

"You and Sue okay now?" Charlie asked. "Only I know she was a bit antsy before. When you took over the other case."

"She's still being a bit of a bitch, to be honest, but I have to try and deal with it and ignoring her doesn't seem to me to be the right thing to do. Actually, she was really lovely when she heard about Serena."

Charlie nodded. "She's got the makings of a good cop. Look, I'm not stupid, and I don't want you to get the wrong idea but, before, when we first took on the angels case, well, I think she had a bit of a thing for me. God, does that sound big-headed?"

"No, I believe you're right. But at the end of the day, you're married, you're a daddy and she's an adult. She just has to get over it. Anyway, I'm giving her a chance. If she doesn't see it for what it is, I'll have her moved. I don't want to, but the case, the team, are what matter."

"Absolutely. Look, you get off. Leave me the details about your niece and I'll ring Edinburgh, see what I can find out and then at least you'll have something to tell your sister. Sounds to me as though your niece has done a runner though. You know, if you take this to Bob Scunthorpe he'll let you go I reckon."

"I know, but I…" Tanya hesitated. "This is going to sound bad, but honestly, I just don't want to go. I'd have to stay with them, I'd be a nuisance to the local bods and I don't see what I can do. I can do better, more important work here. This woman, our victim, she deserves our attention. I was on the spot at the recovery, I saw first-hand what had happened, what she was reduced to – lying in that filthy water. Okay, we don't know much yet, but I want to lead this case."

As she spoke, she had emailed Charlie the notes made during the conversation with Fiona. "Thanks for this, Charlie. Also, could you send Dan and Paul over to the morgue? I've had a text from Dr Hewitt confirming that he's going to do the post-mortem in about an hour. It'll get the information back quicker if they attend, rather than waiting for him to write it up. Tell 'em I'm sorry. It's not going to be nice…"

"Yep. No problem."

"God, Charlie, I don't know how I'd have been able to manage without you at the moment."

"Of course you would. Ah, yes, later you need to tell me about you and Hewitt?"

"How do you mean?"

"Well, Sue said he asked you out."

"When? What the hell is she playing at? She's talking nonsense."

"Okay, okay, she just said that he commented that he wanted to meet up away from a crime scene. She's probably making more of it than it was. I shouldn't have said anything. Look, just forget it."

"No, I bloody won't. I'll have a word with her. Stupid girl. Oh shit, look at the time. I'd better get off. Thanks again, Charlie."

"No problem. Hey, take it easy on Sue, I didn't mean to cause trouble, it was a joke."

"Yeah but… oh, never mind. I'll see you when I get back. What about a drink tonight. If we have a chance."

"Cool, I should make the most of a week of being a bachelor, I'll be back in full husband and daddy mode in no time."

Chapter 10

Once they reached the main road on the way into the city Tanya relaxed into the drive, letting the sat nav guide her. She judged that, away from the office, this might be a time to clear the air between them.

"Couple of things we need to get out in the open, Sue," she said. There was no response. "Okay?"

"Yes... ma'am."

Okay, not a good start but she pressed on. She decided to get the small thing out of the way first. "I've been wondering what you meant. Something you said that puzzled me, about Simon Hewitt."

"Oh, that."

"Yes, I wondered why you made that comment about me, 'Taking him up on it?' Where did that come from?"

She was aware of the other woman staring across the small space between them.

"Are you serious? I mean, not wanting to be rude or anything, but really, are you?" Sue asked.

"Yes." The sat nav indicated a turn, and for a few moments, there was quiet again.

Sue broke the silence. "Well, I reckon that's what he meant. I don't see how it could have been anything else.

When he said about you only ever meeting up at crime scenes, and then he said something like, he'd have to see what you could do about it. I just understood that to mean that he wanted to see you away from work. Well, that's what I would have thought and, to be honest, I wouldn't turn him down. He's a bit tasty, isn't he?"

"Did he really say that?"

"Well, yes. Why would I say he did if it wasn't true? It was when you were looking at the corpse, I think you'd bent down to get a closer look. You didn't answer him, and he just sort of shook his head a bit and then carried on. You really didn't hear him, did you?"

"No, I didn't." It was all that Tanya could think of to say, she was replaying the scene in her mind and truly couldn't remember the comment. "Shit, if he did say that and I just ignored him, well he's going to think I'm a right bitch, isn't he?"

"Well, I don't know. Maybe he thought he'd overstepped the line, with me standing there and all that. Maybe he just thought he'd been unprofessional, although he spoke very quietly, and he was only talking to you. I didn't let on I'd heard."

"Oh hell, that makes it worse, that makes me look like a right tight arse." The sat nav interrupted again. Tanya glanced across the car, if bloody Sue was smirking that was it, she was out. But she wasn't, she was looking down at the phone in her lap, reading an incoming message.

"Okay, I'll have to sort this I suppose, but, and I wouldn't have thought I'd have to say this, Sue, just to be clear, don't go spreading this around. It's personal and I don't want people talking about me behind my back." This was a chance now to test the other woman's loyalty. "You haven't mentioned it to anyone, have you?" The tension between them rose.

"I might have said something to Charlie. Just in passing. You know, him and me were quite close and we sometimes chat."

"Right." Here was the opportunity to settle the rest of the problem. "I know you were working together on the angels case before I was brought in. You didn't make any secret of the fact that you resented my arrival. Me being made the SIO. Charlie was a total professional about it, scored big brownie points with me and more importantly with the DCI. You let it get to you. I'm going to speak plainly, Sue. I know that loyalty to colleagues is vital, but respect for the chain of command is just as important, probably more so actually. Don't be under any misapprehension, in spite of what we are supposed to believe, women still have to work twice as hard to get as far as the men, in this profession as well as any other. We have to be aware all the time what sort of impression we are making. I don't want to have a problem with you.

"Charlie is moving on and you have to as well. Let's just get on and do our job. Let's try to do right by this poor bloody woman, whoever she turns out to be, and you concentrate on being the best you can be. You've got what it takes, but you really need to pull your finger out and stop behaving like a spoiled kid. Okay?" She waited, wondering if the next words from the other woman would be a request for a transfer.

"Yes, boss. Thanks."

As she looked over she saw Sue Rollinson lift a finger and touch the corners of her eyes.

"I've been stupid, I know, but I dug a hole for myself and couldn't get out. I fancied him something rotten you know. I still do," Sue said.

"But there's Carol and little Joshua," Tanya said. "You have to have known it couldn't go anywhere."

To her surprise, Sue laughed.

"I'm a stupid sod sometimes," Sue said.

"Yeah, I guess you are." They had turned into a road of large detached houses. The sat nav told them that they had reached their destination. Tanya parked and turned off the engine. "Are we clear now, Sue?"

"Yes, boss. And boss, thanks. Right, I've had a message from Dan, preliminaries have confirmed it was a woman, she was young or at least youngish and she was dead before the body was burned."

"Thank heavens for that at least." Tanya reached for her bag and followed Sue out of the car and up the wide drive to the detached, mock Tudor house where the Parkers lived. There was a smart, low-slung sports car parked in front of the big double garage and a light shone behind the coloured glass of the front door. Tanya took a breath and raised her finger to the doorbell.

Chapter 11

Julie Parker was taller than either of the two policewomen – blond, blue-eyed and well turned out. She wore slim black trousers and a soft, white blouse with a pattern of butterflies. Tanya recognised the design immediately, she had seen it online, knew the price. She scanned down to the low-heeled shoes and had costed the whole outfit in moments. It was obvious that money was not an issue for this woman and that she treated herself well.

She turned from the door and led them through a spacious hallway and into the kitchen. She indicated the chairs pulled up to a round, oak table. "I hope you don't mind being in here," she said. Her voice was low and soft. She had no discernible accent and Tanya had the feeling that this, along with the classic look, had been deliberately cultivated. She knew that the woman was a successful interior designer and when meeting with clients, appearance would count for a lot. Either looking eccentric and quirky, or affluent and professional, would work with the sort of people who would employ such services and obviously Julie Parker had opted for the second choice.

"Would you like coffee, tea, a cold drink?" she asked, "I've only been back for about fifteen minutes, haven't sorted things out yet."

"No, we're fine, thank you. I'm sorry we have to bother you, Mrs Parker, this must be upsetting for you. We'll try not to take up too much of your time. We will need to speak to your husband of course. Do you have any idea when he'll be back in the country?"

"Yes, apparently, he'll land at Heathrow at nine this evening, if everything is on time. This is his problem, anyway. I don't have anything to do with that business. I suppose it'll all be dealt with by the insurance company, won't it? I'm not sure what it has to do with the police."

"Ah right." Tanya paused a moment. "There is a real possibility that the fire was started deliberately, Mrs Parker, that is one of the reasons that we have become involved."

"Oh God, really. I see." As she answered, Julie Parker sank to a chair, she lowered her eyes for a moment, shook her head. "Well, that's awful. Was it kids, do you think? Druggies? I've told him repeatedly that he should move from there. I mean, it's not a good advert for the business anyway, it's rough. Well, maybe now he'll listen. Bloody hell, arson, it could really screw up the insurance claim."

"I wonder if you could explain for us exactly what it is your husband uses the warehouse for?"

"Well, as I say I don't have anything to do with the business, but really it's just his storage place. He sources cars you see. Special cars to order for clients. You know the sort of thing, penis extensions for Arabs." Covering her mouth with her hand Julie blushed, "Sorry, I probably shouldn't have said that."

"It's okay, I guess it describes what he does pretty clearly." Tanya smiled, and the other woman grinned back.

She paused for a moment, the next questions could be difficult; could lead to genuine grief. She opened her notebook, playing for time. Sue was silent and still beside her. "Who works with your husband at the warehouse?"

In response the other woman shook her head again, her mouth turned down at the corners. "Nobody really. He has some people who work for him, here, out in the Middle East, America, Australia, but they are all self-employed contractors, mostly working to source vehicles or find customers, a lot of it on the internet. They are go-betweens I suppose, and he does the co-ordination. Organises shipping, puts the men with the cars that they can't live without." She gave a short huff of a laugh. "He has a couple of delivery drivers as well; again they are casual, he just uses them as he needs them. He prefers to drive the cars himself if possible. That's his thing really, the business gives him an excuse to play with fast cars."

"Are they men or women? The drivers."

"I'm not sure. The ones I have met have all been men. They change though, I don't know who he has at the moment. Why?"

Tanya closed the notebook and folded her hands on top of the oak table, "Is there anyone that you think might have been in the warehouse while your husband was away? A cleaner maybe, an accountant, secretary?"

"No, nobody. His accountant is freelance, she works at home, and he does the office paperwork himself. Ah, so you have who did it. Is that what you're telling me?"

As she spoke they could see her begin to join the dots, her face paled under the carefully applied cosmetics. "Oh, either that or... No, you're not saying that somebody was in there when it went up, are you? When the police rang Cornwall, they said it was badly damaged, a big fire."

Tanya didn't answer.

"Are they alright? I mean I can't imagine who it might be. He's away and the place is always locked and secure. As I said it's a rough area. So, are they okay? No, they can't be. If they were, you wouldn't be asking these questions." They sat quietly as she reached the inevitable conclusion.

Tanya spoke quietly, "Unfortunately, there was an individual in the building and they did not survive."

"How terrible. Is it the person who started the fire then? It must be, mustn't it?"

"We don't think so, no."

Julie Parker's face was creased with confusion. She flicked her glance between the two policewomen. "I don't understand what you're saying. There wasn't supposed to be anyone in the warehouse. If there was, then they were up to something, and if there was a fire then, well, it stands to reason that they were the ones who started it. Surely, that's obvious."

Tanya glanced at Sue Rollinson before she spoke. "We don't have a lot of information at the moment. What we do have is a deceased person who we believe is a woman, not very old. She was found at the scene and her body is badly damaged by the effects of the fire. Now, you have told me that there is no one that you can think of who should have been there." She paused, and Julie Parker nodded, her eyes were wide with shock and her hand, when she raised it to her mouth, was shaking.

Tanya continued. "Obviously the first thing we would like to do is to find out who this is, and then, we will have to discover why they were in a locked and secure area."

"I don't know, I just don't know."

The woman was distressed, and it didn't seem that she was going to be able to give them any more information, not right then. Tanya decided that they had done all that they could for the time being. "Well, thank you for your time, Mrs Parker. Obviously, the next thing we will have to do is speak to your husband and, hopefully, he'll be able to shed some more light on this. In the meantime, just keep this to yourself. Our investigations are at the very early stages. Will you let us know when your husband is back home, or maybe he could call us himself?" She held out a business card and the other woman took it from her with shaking fingers, turning it back and forth on the top of the table.

"Yes, I'll get him to call you." She glanced down at the small white card, "Detective Inspector. It might be late."

"Well, in the circumstances it's probably best if he gives us a call in the morning and we can arrange a time to have a chat with him." Tanya smiled and pushed the chair back from the table. Sue stood and walked to the kitchen door. "I'm sorry if this has been disturbing for you, Mrs Parker. Hopefully we'll be able to clear things up quite quickly. We'll find our own way out, don't disturb yourself."

As they left the bright, clean kitchen she looked back to see Julie Parker lower her face into her hands.

Chapter 12

Back in the car, Tanya retraced the earlier route, struggling with the Friday traffic. After a couple of minutes spent entering notes into her tablet, Sue clicked the sleep button and turned to look across the car. "She doesn't seem to think much of the hubbie's job, does she?" she said.

"No, I thought that too. Then again, at least one of them is making good money. That kitchen was lovely, and did you see the coffee maker? Top of the range, and her clothes were pretty sharp. I nearly bought a blouse like that one she was wearing. It wasn't cheap, I went for a striped one instead." She didn't note Sue's raised eyebrows and would not have understood anyway.

"I haven't had a chance yet to check her company website, have you had a look?" Tanya asked.

"No, Kate did the research. By all accounts, it's pretty impressive. She has some well-known clients and she organises everything from whole house make-overs to small decorative jobs. She could be making a good living, I suppose. It's not the sort of world we'd know much about, is it?"

Tanya visualised her own newly decorated house, the carefully designed dressing room with its rows of cupboards and wardrobes. She had a good idea just how much custom design cost. "No, I guess not," she said.

They were not getting very far. They were no nearer to identifying the victim, and hadn't been able to interview the property owner.

"Get me the details of the 999 call, will you? I was waiting for the fire officer, but we'll just get onto that ourselves. I need details of the person who raised the alarm. It was a bloke, he might have noticed something that'll help." She knew that she should also talk directly with Simon Hewitt and the thought of facing him, after Sue's comments, made her stomach flip. Another complication that she could do without.

"Okay." Sue made a note. After a pause she said, "Have you heard anything more about your niece? Samantha, is it?"

"Serena." Tanya felt a flash of irritation, but it was tinged with guilt. Honestly, she had forgotten about the other drama and knew that she shouldn't have done. Shouldn't problems with family be uppermost in her mind? She answered that she had asked Charlie to see what he could find out, that he was going to contact the force in Scotland looking for information. As she spoke she knew that she was trying to give the impression she was involved and affording the matter the attention it deserved. Now, when she had been forced to think about it, she was just a little worried because a young girl was missing, but only in the way that she would be about anyone's daughter, only in the way that they all were when they scanned the Misper lists. It was obvious from the concerned expression on her passenger's face that she had expected more.

"Well, if I can do anything just let me know. Why don't you take some time? I'm sure the DCI would let you go up there. He can re-allocate this job."

There it was again, this idea that she should leave her life and dash to the aid of her sister. The irritation grew, she snapped back, "I think that this is possibly more important than a teenaged tantrum though, don't you, Sue?" There was silence from the other side of the car and she felt the tension rising again.

Chapter 13

Charlie was in the office, sitting at the smaller desk – the one that had been Tanya's.

He looked up as she came in and waved a small wad of pages at her. "These are the print-outs from Edinburgh. The steps they've taken and the record of the interview with your sister. You can see she was very upset."

Tanya scanned the text. Her sister had been antagonistic and complaining. Typical Fiona. The constable sent to talk to her about Serena had been professional and as reasonable as she could be in the face of Fiona's attitude. But, in fairness, her sister didn't know where her daughter was, and Tanya couldn't really begin to understand what that must feel like. Perhaps on this occasion her attitude had been understandable.

The girl had left for college at the usual time. There had been no arguments, according to Fiona at least. When she was late home, friends who were contacted had all said that she had seemed perfectly normal during the day. She hadn't travelled on the usual bus home, however, but left to walk by a different route. Clothes were missing from her wardrobe. It wasn't possible to say what exactly. According to her mother, the girl shopped for her own things and it was mostly in black: jeans, hoodies and the occasional dress or band T-shirt. Therefore she had no real idea of what might be missing. The only evidence that everything wasn't there was the number of empty hangers. Her phone was in the drawer of her bedside cabinet and, yes, Fiona had agreed that was very odd. It was turned off. The police had it in the IT department but as the SIM card had been removed it was just about useless: no more than a pretty plastic case; even the call history had been deleted.

Because she was under eighteen they had listed her on the missing persons register but she wasn't considered particularly vulnerable and to all intents and purposes appeared to have left of her own accord. On the mother's insistence, they had removed her computer and were in the process of investigating her search history and emails. However, it looked as though the girl was pretty clued up and the machine had been cleaned out thoroughly. It was going to take some time to extract information from the hard drive. The worry, of course, was that she had been groomed by an older person, probably a man, and lured away. As she read the reports, Tanya had to swallow down the first stirring of real fear. From her experience in the missing persons department she could see that this was a real possibility.

She glanced up at Charlie and saw her worry reflected in his face. "Shit. This doesn't look like a bit of a strop does it, Charlie?"

"It doesn't. What are you going to do, Tanya? I have to say the locals are doing all that they can, but what about your sister? She probably needs you up there right now, don't you think?"

Tanya sighed and swung her chair around to face the window. "She's got her husband, the other kids. It's not like she's on her own."

She sounded petulant to her own ears and when she spun back to face Charlie she could see disapproval on his face, and something else. Disappointment? Her mind was racing, torn between this embryonic case of arson and murder and the pull of what were admittedly weak family ties, she knew what she really wanted to do.

Charlie spoke, quietly: "Look, why don't you take this to the DCI? I have a suggestion. I'm going to be around at least until the end of next week. You could go up to Scotland, reassure your sister that you're monitoring things up there. You won't be able to do much more than has already been done, I know. But she'll feel better and I think you will as well. In the meantime, if Bob Scunthorpe agrees, and it won't cause too many administrative problems, I could work with the team here until you get back. I'd keep you totally up to date and you could just slot back in when your niece is safely home. What do you reckon?"

Tanya could see that if she didn't act now, the tenuous connection with the only remaining family she had would be lost. She wondered just how bad that would be. Did she really care? If they were no longer a part of her life would it be much of a loss anyway? However, somewhere buried deep inside her was a residual loyalty to her parents who only came to value her much too late in their own lives, and to a sister who had shared her childhood, albeit from the dizzy heights of the favourite daughter.

Tanya stood and took a couple of steps towards the door. "Let's go and have a word with him, if he's available, and then I'll give you the rundown on Julie Parker. Alan Parker is due back tonight and I was planning to see him tomorrow. Sue can fill you in on the rest."

As they walked down the corridor, Tanya felt the weight of family duty on her shoulders in a way that she never had before, and more than anything else, it made her angry.

Chapter 14

Tanya had known what the outcome of a meeting with her boss would be. He told her that she should go to Scotland to support her sister. He promised to contact his counterpart in the Edinburgh force, to arrange for Tanya to meet the people who were dealing with the situation. He was a little less sure about the suggestion that Charlie Lambert take temporary charge of the arson case.

"It seems a bit messy," he said. "What if Merseyside sort out the problems with your transfer in a couple of days, and they need you up there?"

They all knew that the obvious solution was to give the investigation to another team. For them, Paul Harris, as a detective sergeant, could have been placed in temporary charge, under supervision, but although he was thorough and dogged when assigned to something, he lacked the spark of imagination that could make all the difference. Bob Scunthorpe looked at Tanya's worried, hopeful face and he felt for her. He understood the struggle between her keenness to work for the dead woman from the warehouse, and the pull of duty to her sister's family.

"How long do you think you'll need?" he asked.

"A couple of days. Just to reassure her really, let her know everything is being done that can be, sir," Tanya said.

"Leave it with me. I'll have a word with the Merseyside Force and see what we can sort out between us. But your house is sold, isn't it, Charlie? Where will you live, if you have to stay on a while? You can't want to go into the section house, even if there is space."

Tanya spoke out, "It's not a problem, sir, he can stay at my place. I've got a spare room and, anyway, I won't be there, will I?"

"Thanks, Tanya." Charlie grinned at her. "To be honest our place is pretty grim just now, I've been sleeping on a camp bed. It'll be nice to be in a proper home."

Bob Scunthorpe picked up his phone. "Okay, go and get things organised, but Charlie, it could be that the only way to do this is to keep you here until the case is sorted."

"No problem, sir. Carol is happy at her sister's and she has company all the time, help with the baby, it might work out for the best in the long run."

Bob began to dial. "Right, let me see what's what. Tanya…"

She turned on the way to the door.

"If there is anything I can do, just let me know. I hope this is all a storm in a teacup, but if it's not…" He hesitated. "Well, let's all just hope for the best, shall we?"

"Yes, sir. Thank you."

"Charlie, keep me in the loop."

"Sir."

They brought the team up to date. Sue hid her smile behind a hand and blushed when she saw Tanya's raised eyebrow.

Tanya and Charlie drove in tandem to her house. She had the times of the trains and was planning to buy her ticket at the station. She called her sister and arranged to be met at Waverley Station. All there was left to do was pack and settle Charlie in her house.

She didn't want to do any of it. She liked Charlie a lot, but her home was her castle. It had been rented through an agent while she was away, but now she was back; she had reclaimed it. It had been refurbished and remodelled to make it the special place that she wanted to live. As she gave him 'the tour' explained the security system and the kitchen appliances she had a knot of unhappiness in her belly. She didn't show him her dressing room, it wasn't somewhere he would need to go and, though she constantly told herself that her shopping and her wardrobe, were her affair, she acknowledged the little seed of embarrassment at the evidence of her personal extravagance.

Charlie wasn't stupid, he picked up on her mood. "I'll take care of it, Tanya. No wild parties, I promise."

She managed to summon a grin for him. "Oh, I know you will, mate, it's just that I don't really want to do any of this. I know it's the right thing, I know I don't have much choice, but it really does rankle. Bloody Serena, why the hell couldn't she just have got pregnant if she wanted to cause a drama. Oh sorry, that was a stupid thing to say. You will keep me up to date on the Jane Doe though, won't you? Ring me every day and immediately if there's anything important. And when you've seen Dr Hewitt give me a call and if you could record the interview with Alan Parker, send me a copy."

"Yes, I will. I promise. Anyway look, you'll be back by the end of the weekend I'll bet and send me back to my hovel."

She nodded glumly and turned away to head for the stairs. "I'll pack my stuff and get an Uber to the station."

"I can take you."

"No, it's fine." As she spoke she opened the Uber app and began to order a car. "What!" She held the phone away from her, staring at the screen. "Oh, for god's sake. I'd forgotten about that."

"What?" Charlie asked.

"This card, there's a problem with it. I had trouble in the restaurant. I meant to sort it out but then we caught the case."

"Well, you need to do that pretty soon. If you leave it, the bank can be stroppy about repaying any money that you lose. What's the problem with it? Has the account been hacked?"

"I don't know, it just says rejected. Oh look, I'll have to do it on the way. I'll ring the helpline. I haven't time now. Is the offer of a lift still open?"

"Yes, of course. But you need to hurry, you don't want to miss the train on top of everything else."

She clomped up the stairs muttering to herself. "Bloody Serena. Soddin' Fiona."

Charlie grinned, but he also said a silent prayer that Tanya's family would not be riven with grief.

Chapter 15

Fiona parked in New Street and gave her sister directions by phone, as Tanya dragged her suitcase behind her through the late night city. She had visited before, of course, and liked Edinburgh, but tonight the only thing she wanted was to be heading in the other direction, to be going home, the problem with her niece sorted, her duty done.

She had spent much of the journey talking on her phone. At the last minute she had decided to travel first class, paying with her second credit card and feeling grateful that she had more than one piece of plastic. Now that it had been forced back into her mind, she had known she would need to sort the bank problem by phone, quickly if possible. Not something she could do in a crowded carriage, and she convinced herself that she needed privacy anyway, in case Charlie rang with news about the case. By the time she reached Scotland, she was regretting the extravagance.

Charlie did ring, but not with much news, just to let her know that the team had gone home. Dan and Paul had come back from the post-mortem and told them that evidence of blunt trauma to the back of the skull had been confirmed, and it was most probably the cause of death. This effectively ruled out any chance of an accident, so he was meeting with the medical examiner first thing in the morning, but a report was being typed up before then. He would also see Alan Parker before noon. The main development was a figure seen on the closed circuit recording. It was a decent image and the beat officers were touring the clubs and bars. They had traced the man who had raised the fire alarm. Dan had arranged to go and see him, just in case there was anything else he could tell them. Charlie wanted to chat, she did not but couldn't swerve it without being rude.

He asked the inevitable question. "Did you sort things with your bank card?"

"Oh yeah. That's fine." As she lied, nausea turned her stomach and she felt cold sweat on her forehead, stickiness under her arms. She couldn't tell him, couldn't tell anyone, that she had overspent on her card so much that the bank was threatening to cancel all her plastic. She had no overdraft arrangement and the leeway that they had given her was going to cost a fortune. Every day the fine would increase until payday, still a week away when she would, possibly, clear the overspend, but not her credit debt. She hadn't been able to access her bank accounts on the train because the security settings of the sites withheld approval on 4G connections. She had been horrified by what she had been told, had argued that there must be some mistake at their end, but she would log on as soon as she had a secure line, and see just what had happened. She'd jotted down her recent spending, the stuff she could immediately remember, and with a surge of acid in her belly, determined that maybe it wasn't a mistake by the bank after all.

She had cancelled three outstanding orders immediately but was disgusted with herself for letting things get so very far out of hand. Now that she no longer had the income from renting out her house, and with the expense of the redecoration, plus the treats she had bought herself, well, her money was spent. She had passed through panic and settled into hoping that when she looked, it would not be as bad as she feared.

When her sister stepped from her car and she saw Fiona's ravaged features, took in her dishevelled appearance, she knew it would be a while before she would be able to get back to this new and frightening problem.

Fiona's eyes were red and puffy, she wore no makeup and, instead of the usual cold, air kiss that marked their meetings, she had leapt from the car and wrapped her arms around Tanya, clinging to her while she sobbed into her shoulder.

"Hey. Come on, calm down, Fi. It's okay, I'm here now and we'll soon have this sorted."

"We have to find her, we have to find her tonight. I don't know where my little girl is. I want her home. Tanya, find her for me."

Of everything that had happened, this total breakdown of her sister's cool exterior was the most shocking. Tanya helped Fiona back into the car, taking the keys.

"Let me drive, you're in no state. Come on, Fi, get a grip."

As they turned out of the car park, she patted her sister's knee. "Come on, it's going to be fine. We'll fix this," she said. But now, with the situation suddenly become starkly visible, Tanya's concern had increased. This was real, this was happening.

Chapter 16

The younger children had been farmed out, staying with school friends for the weekend at least. Graham was quiet. He sat in his big leather chair before the dead fire, his head lowered, his hands in fists on his lap. He had nodded at Tanya as she walked into the room. Just a one-word greeting was all that he managed. His eyes had swum with moisture and he turned away.

"He's just got in," Fiona said. "He's been out, walking the streets, all the places we know that she goes. The shopping mall until it closed, the cafés and bars, clubs. Oh, we know she goes to places where she's not supposed to – they all do. They have fake ID."

"You know this, and you haven't done anything?" Tanya was shocked at the seeming lack of parental control. "You let her do stuff like that?"

Fiona chewed her lips. "It looks bad, I see that, but it's so hard, Tanya; nobody prepares you for this crap. They hand you a baby and that's it, that's it forever and you do the best that you can. You want to make them happy and when they're Serena's age they can only be happy when they're the same as all their friends. She had a curfew, and she kept to it, up until now anyway." She paused for a moment, gasped out a sob and wiped her eyes.

"We trusted her, we thought that if we treated her like an adult she'd behave like one. She never came home drunk, nothing like that. We thought we were getting it right. I didn't want it to be like it was for me, for us. Me, always in early to do my homework, always in bed before ten because there was school in the morning, music class, language school, extra tuition. I know they weren't as strict with you, I envied you that." She couldn't continue but perched on the edge of the sofa and let the tears come.

"You envied me! I always reckoned it was because they didn't really care what I did, where I went. As long as I wasn't causing trouble, they were glad to have me out from under their feet."

Tanya stopped speaking. This wasn't the time, there would probably never be a time when there was any point in going over it. Their parents were dead, and it was all in the past. The reality of Fiona's childhood had been very different to Tanya's own, but maybe it wasn't quite what she had thought it was. She shrugged, she had spent years trying to let it go and didn't want it all brought back. She was surprised though, it had seemed that Fiona had it all under control: the job, the motherhood, life in Scotland among what Tanya could only ever think of as posh friends; and yet here was her sister, admitting to being vulnerable and insecure. But of course she was, her daughter was missing, she was scared stupid. Once this was all sorted the situation would revert to the way that it had always been, Fiona with the glittering prizes and Tanya constantly trying to prove herself. She tried to calm things a bit, bring the tension down.

"Anyway, I never did much – no clubs, no bars." She gave a short laugh. "No money. You can't do much with no money." There was no response.

Tanya looked at them, her only living relatives – these people that she hardly knew – broken and devastated and realised that the only way she would help them was to step back, to be what she was, to do what she did well.

"Okay, I'm going to bed and you should as well." She was ready for the shocked expression, the shaking of heads, she had seen it before in other houses, with other parents. "Look, she's not coming back tonight. There's nothing we can do right now, the police are aware of her, they will be watching in the streets. It's too dark to look any more and I need to sleep. I can't function well when I'm dead on my feet. I'm having a few hours and then I'll go through everything, right from the start, I'll talk to my colleagues at the local station and then I'll find Serena. Okay?"

It was a foolish promise, weakly rooted in emotion, and Tanya knew it for a mistake as soon as she had spoken. What she didn't say was how long it might take, where the girl might be when they found her, and in what state. But right then, she meant it, she would sort this, it was something that she knew how to do.

"Come on, have you got any sleeping pills, anything like that?"

Fiona shook her head. "I don't use them."

"Well, okay then, we'll all go to bed. You need to rest. We have to go through everything tomorrow and I need you both thinking clearly. Come on."

Tanya stood up and held out a hand. Graham shook his head. "Sorry, I can't. The very idea of getting into bed when I don't know where she is, appals me. It's okay. I'll sleep here, by the phone." He lifted the handsfree and waved it at them. "I'll see you later."

Tanya helped her sister upstairs and left her outside the door to the guest room. It was only when she heard the click of the door handle to the master suite that she remembered her bag, still in the hall, beside the stairs. She went back down. The door to the lounge was ajar, a slender bar of light streaked across the carpet. She heard her brother-in-law speaking low and quiet. She didn't hesitate for long but stepped back quietly and stood in the dim hallway listening.

He said, "Fiona's sister's here now, I don't know what she thinks she can do. I'm at the end of my tether, I want to see you. Meet me, meet me tomorrow and we'll talk about what we do now."

She heard him arrange a time and she heard him murmur endearments. She thought of her sister upstairs, more than likely crying into her pillow, and her heart sank because this was another complication. She wasn't a fool, she knew what she had heard.

Chapter 17

The alarm was set for five-thirty, but Tanya was already awake when it started to bleep. She could hear movement in the house, the drumming of water in the shower, doors opening and closing. She didn't imagine that Fiona had been able to sleep much, but at least they had a break from each other and the desperate anxiety.

It was too early to call Charlie Lambert, but she checked her email just in case. Nothing had happened overnight, which wasn't a surprise. She sent him a message: 'Send me everything as soon as you have it. Things are pretty bad up here, but I'll fit it all in'.

Graham had made coffee and he turned as she walked into the kitchen, dressed in jeans and hoodie but with her feet bare. He gave her a rueful smile.

"I'm sorry. I was pretty rude last night," he said. "I just want to say thanks for coming. I really appreciate it. I don't know what you can do really but having someone on the inside – sort of thing – it feels good. You'll be able to make sure they don't take their eye off the ball. I know it appears that Serena left on her own, but it's so unlike her and…"

He shrugged and turned to the window. He placed his hands on the edge of the worktop, his arms braced as he leaned forward, his head lowered. "I just want her back. Once she's back we can sort out any problems, you know, work out why she's done this. We had no clue, no idea that she was so unhappy."

"Are you sure?" Tanya said.

He turned to look at her, a frown lowering his dark eyebrows. "How do you mean? Of course, I'm sure."

"I've had some experience, well, you know that and sometimes, actually quite often in a case like this, the clues have been there and have just been missed by the family. That's something I want to do today, I want to get into the real ins and outs of your lives. Things that might not seem important to you, or didn't at the time, but could be a clue to what was going on in her life. She left for a reason and I reckon she probably had a destination in mind when she went."

"We've checked her accounts, there was nothing. Fiona is the joint account holder, with Serena being too young to open one on her own. That was one of the first things we did. She hadn't bought tickets or anything as far as we could tell," Graham said.

"I need to look at the statements later. If you could print them out for me that will help."

Tanya poured coffee and took a piece of toast from the plate on the table. She looked up at Graham. She was waiting, holding onto her knowledge from last night. It was still just possible there was an innocent explanation for what she had heard, and if so then he would be telling them, or at least telling Fiona, where he was going, who he was meeting. No point stirring up the waters, the atmosphere was already charged and brittle.

Fiona came into the room. Her long hair was still damp, pulled back from her face in a ponytail. She poured a drink and sat at the table, opposite to Tanya.

"Right, let's get on with this," she said.

The brusqueness of her tone, the no-nonsense look on her face was reassuring. This was the Fiona that Tanya could work with, the helpless mess of the previous evening was too much of a stranger; her sister was back, maybe not in appearance, but the steel was back in her nerves.

Tanya opened her laptop and clicked on the folder she had labelled 'Serena'. "Send me copies of her bank statements and then I want to see any homework books, any diaries, anything like that. I need to go through her room."

"They already did that, the other officers," Graham said.

"Yes, I know, and I've seen the reports, but I need to see for myself to get a feel for it all." She paused. "All credit to the local force but they might have missed something."

Tanya's laptop beeped, she glanced at the screen. "Oh, I need to read this. Won't be long." Her fingers flew across the keyboard, she was aware of them both watching her. She looked up and shook her head. "It's nothing, it's about my other case. A report from Charlie."

"Your other case?" She saw immediately the glint in her sister's eyes. Her stomach knotted. She should have told them straight away, but she simply hadn't, she wasn't used to sharing information about her life. She nodded. "Yes, the arson case I'm working on."

"But you're not doing that now. You're here to help us now, aren't you?" Fiona was frowning.

"Yes, of course I am, but I'm running this as well. It's fine, we've got it sorted. I just need to read this, it's a report from the medical examiner and I might need to act on it." She saw the fury flare, the look of disbelief.

"You can't be serious. Your niece is missing. My little girl has vanished and you're putting it aside to deal with some dead stranger. I don't believe this. Tell me, why exactly have you come?" As Fiona railed at her Graham crossed the kitchen and put his arms around his wife.

"Hey, come on. Don't get like this."

"Don't get like this! Look at her, here we are in the middle of trying to work out just what's happened with Serena and she breaks off, my sister, her aunt, breaks off to talk to some medical examiner."

"No, I'm not talking to him, this is just the report. I'm just reading the report. It's fine, honestly it's fine."

Fiona stood up and turned towards the door. "I should have known, I should have known that we would never be important enough for you to leave your precious career, your precious job. Christ, we've never mattered to you, have we? I don't know why you've come if all you're going to do is carry on with your other work." She stormed from the room, Graham pounding after her and she heard them running up the stairs and then the slam of the bedroom door.

For a moment there was quiet. Tanya sat in the empty room, the click and tick of the radiator as the heating came on and the chirp of birds in the garden were the only noise now. She paused for just a moment before turning back to her laptop and opening the file from Charlie, she dragged her notebook across the table, flipped over the page and picked up her pen.

Chapter 18

The report was as Tanya had expected and the cold, precise delivery gave no indication of the reality of what it must have been like for the two detectives observing the examination. She felt sorry for Dan and Paul when she read the description of the burned and fragile skin, the body fat melted away, the eyes – boiled, burned, burst. It must have been grim in the morgue. The heat had been insufficient to carbonize the bones, and though this was a blessing for them in the gathering of evidence, it was a relief to know for certain that the woman had been dead when the flames had engulfed her. This was confirmed by the lack of any inhalation of smoke or burning of the inside of the throat and lungs.

She highlighted parts of the document, and copied and pasted others into her own notes. It was a portrayal of the deceased, cobbled together from sad remains. The woman's height and her estimated age, the fact that she was probably a little undernourished. Simon Hewitt had sent away tissue and blood samples to be tested for drug abuse. No tattoos or scars on the unburned parts of the body, no chance of fingerprints. Nothing much to help them, unless the DNA results brought a miracle. She knew better than to hope for too much. They were reaching out to dentists but the teeth had a few old fillings and nothing that looked recent.

Tanya wrote an email to Charlie. She thanked him, told him that things in Scotland were tricky and left it at that.

Above her were raised voices, the slam of doors and when someone thundered down the stairs she walked to the kitchen door. Fiona was dressed for outside, a padded gilet over her sweater.

"Are you going out?" Tanya asked.

Fiona spat the words at her sister, "Yes, I'm going out. I'm going out to look for your niece. You don't seem to have fully grasped this, Detective Inspector Miller," there was anger and pain behind the words, "but my little girl is missing, and someone has to find her."

Tanya drew in a breath. "Where are you going to go?"

"What?"

"You've looked everywhere already. Several times, you've been around and around the area, gone to her friends, her college, her usual haunts. You haven't found her. You won't find her, not wandering about without a plan."

She waited, watched Fiona's face crumple and her shoulders slump and then she moved across the small distance between them and wrapped her arms around her sister and held her close while she sobbed and sniffed. Fiona eventually lifted her head and from somewhere deep inside she dredged up a watery smile.

"What should I do then?" she asked.

"You should come in here with me, and we should go over everything and then we should go up to her room and turn it inside out because somewhere there is the explanation for all of this."

"And your dead woman, the other case?" Fiona pointed to the laptop, still open on the kitchen table.

"I've told you, I can handle this. Charlie is brilliant and, with his help, I can do that, and this. Have some faith in me, Fiona, I've got this. I know how to do my job. All my jobs."

Chapter 19

It took most of the morning to turn out cupboards and drawers. Fiona insisted that she had already looked everywhere. Tanya nodded and carried on. She conducted the search the way that she had learned. This way had, in the past, unearthed hidden letters, secreted diaries and even in one case a laptop that the parents of a fourteen-year-old boy didn't know existed. Serena's violin was in its padded backpack propped against the wall. Fiona picked it up and fiddled with the zip.

"I hadn't realised that some days I just don't even come into her room. She was supposed to have a music lesson after school. I should have noticed that she hadn't taken this. If I had done, then maybe this would never have happened. Or at least I might have called her, taken it to her or something and then I would have known. I would, wouldn't I?"

She paused and sighed. "It all seemed so good, you know? All so well organised and peaceful. I don't understand where I've gone wrong."

She sat for a while longer with the instrument case on her lap, gazing out of the window at the big back garden. Tanya could think of nothing to say that would help, so she carried on, turning out drawers, examining the undersides of cabinets and pulling up the edges of the carpet.

By lunchtime, it seemed likely that they had exhausted every avenue and she called a break.

"I just need a few minutes to talk to Charlie," Tanya told Fiona. She waited for an outburst, but none came. Her sister seemed to have accepted the working arrangement. Graham had said that he was going out to walk the streets. Tanya hadn't commented, it wasn't her business unless his secrets had something to do with Serena, and for now that wasn't clear.

* * *

Charlie had been to see Alan Parker. "Odd bloke to be honest," he told Tanya, "definitely punching above his weight with that wife."

"Was he any help?"

"Not really. He was away, wasn't he? Said that he had no idea who could have been in the warehouse, nobody should have been. He thought it was all secure. The two cars that were in there were on order for a couple of clients in Australia and to be honest, he seemed more upset about those than he did about the fact that somebody had died in his property."

"You didn't like him, did you?"

"Is it that obvious? No, I didn't. There was something about him that was just a bit off. But then again, in real terms he is just a used car salesman, isn't he?"

"Bit of a cliché there, Charlie." Tanya laughed.

"Yes, I suppose so. But he wasn't the sort of bloke you could take to, if you know what I mean. He didn't seem particularly concerned about the woman. He didn't ask any questions about her; couldn't suggest who she might have been. I had the impression he was more worried about the insurance cover. He asked a few times about a crime number and how soon he could have access. I guess the cars were worth a small fortune and that's possibly lost now. Anyway, the paperwork for the cars should be in the office, whenever we can get in there.

"I was surprised that he didn't have any electronic records, but he said he prefers hard copies. The fire officer reckons the place will be safe for workmen to get into later today and then they should be able to fix some sort of temporary access to the mezzanine. Not sure how safe it's going to be until someone does a survey. Don't see how much it's going to tell us though. I don't know if they are important, but we need to look."

He was quiet for a minute and in the background there was the hum of voices. The sound made Tanya long for her office and the incident room.

"Some good news though. There is someone on the CCTV."

"Is it the bloke who raised the alarm? Have you spoken to him yet?"

"Dan and Paul have. Not much there I don't think. He was on his way home from the pub and saw the smoke. He called it in; that was it. He hung around until the brigade turned up and then he was ushered away with everyone else. Old bloke; fairly matter of fact about it all. Anyway, there is this other man. Not a bad image and we've got a print-out doing the rounds of the clubs and bars."

"Great stuff, Charlie. I'll wait to hear back about that. It feels like a step forward at least."

"I'm sending you a recording of the Parker interview. I couldn't get visual, not in his own house, but you can listen. Any movement up there?"

"Not much. I'm going later today to speak to a Detective Laird and will probably ask about a television appeal. Maybe if Serena is staying somewhere with a boy or something like that and she sees the state her mum is in, she might get in touch. We can hope anyway. Thanks, Charlie. I'll ring you later."

She rang off and filled in her notes. Her spirits lifted a little, there had been a few tiny steps forward. She desperately wanted to be there. Things sometimes broke suddenly and if that happened she needed to be a part of it, properly not just virtually. She thought they'd got everything covered but at one removed she worried something run of the mill might be missed.

Chapter 20

It had to be done. So, while the house was quiet, Tanya sat on the end of the bed and made a call to the bank. Late the night before, before she could give in to sleep, and because everything was already such a mess, she didn't see how it could possibly get any worse so she had logged onto the website. She had been wrong; it got worse. There was no mistake by the bank, there were no problems with her cards except that they were maxed out. She had done some quick calculations and the stark truth was, even after payday, once her bills were settled, she would immediately slide back into the red.

The advisor who answered the phone sounded impossibly young. His tone was polite but cold. Together they went through her options and before she rang off she had arranged an overdraft. She tried to convince him that charging her for every day she had been overdrawn was only making the situation worse, that it was nonsensical, but he wouldn't be moved.

She finished the call and threw the phone across the bed. She was angry mostly with herself. Even after her salary was deposited, she would have to cut back on her spending and monitor her outgoings. She had never had an overdraft before, but with her plastic strained to breaking point, there was no choice and having to keep a check on her spending was depressing.

Her parents had struggled for as long as she could remember – going without to make sure that Fiona had all she needed. She had been their great white hope, the one thing that they could be proud of, but they had all suffered for it, Tanya most of all. Determined that she would have a good, well-paid job, she'd put everything into it, climbing the ranks and intending to go as high as possible. A good salary now and a decent pension guaranteed. Now here she was: in debt and worse off than Mum and Dad had ever been. They always paid their rent on time and the electric and gas had been through a coin meter, no chance of a bill they couldn't cover. They would have never borrowed money, never gone into the red with the bank. Tears of fury and disappointment pricked at the back of her eyes. This was self-inflicted. Constant online shopping and lack of discipline had brought her to this. She was disgusted with herself.

The front door slammed, and Graham's voice drifted up from the hallway. She stood up and smoothed down her sweater. She'd fix it, cut back for a couple of months and it would be fine. In the meantime, there were more important things to think about.

As she passed the door to Serena's pretty bedroom she stepped inside. Everything was just what one would expect. Fairy lights wound into the headboard; band pictures and selfies with friends printed out and pinned to the walls. On the desk in front of the window there was nothing, just a slight difference in the colour of the wood where the laptop should have been. The violin case was still at the bottom of the bed where Fiona had sat cradling it.

Tanya knew little about music. She listened sometimes in the car, but it wasn't a big thing in her life. She knew even less about violins. She unzipped the case and stroked a finger across the shining surface. The interior of the backpack was a moulded form with the violin itself fitting snugly inside. Tanya curled her fingers around the neck and tried to lift it out. She hadn't loosened the small padded flap that held the thing in place and as she tugged she felt the inside cradle move and shift, detaching from the cover. She jerked her hand away. She had no idea how much these things cost, but for sure it didn't look cheap, and she didn't think it was supposed to come apart like this. She pushed at the moulded polystyrene. It wouldn't settle back neatly into the case, she pressed around the edges with her fingertips, but it was twisted, standing proud. She would have to take it out fully and reinsert it. She heard the soft thud of feet on the stairs. This was going to be embarrassing. With a glance behind, she moved to stand between the half-open door and the bed. She tugged at the insert again and it lifted out quite readily. Underneath, partly wedged against the side, was a small white envelope. She picked it up between her thumb and forefinger. A quick shiver of excitement ran down her spine. As Fiona stepped into the room Tanya held the envelope in front of her.

"I think I may have found something," she said.

* * *

The envelope was in one small evidence bag and the small pile of white pills was in another. Tanya, Fiona, and Graham sat around the kitchen table with the plastic bags between them. Fiona reached out with one finger and pushed the packet of pills towards her sister.

"Do you know for certain, though?" she asked. "They could be something else, couldn't they?"

"No, I don't know for certain," Tanya said. "All I can tell you is that I have seen these before, they are quite distinctive with the butterfly logo on them. We seized some a while ago at a club – they came from The Netherlands. But until the lab has been able to examine

73

them, we won't know for certain. I believe that they are Ecstasy though. Look at it logically, if they were aspirin, which they patently are not, then they would hardly be hidden in the bottom of a violin case, would they?"

"Maybe they got in there by accident. Perhaps they slid in…"

Tanya didn't bother to answer, they all knew that it was nonsense – the pills had been deliberately hidden.

Graham spoke quietly, "So what do we do next? How will this help us to find her? Do we have to tell the police?"

"Well, yes of course we have to tell them," Tanya said. "You know that. But I'll do it. I have my meeting in about an hour with Detective Laird. How it will help… well, I don't know. The envelope looks ordinary, we'll fingerprint it of course but I can't imagine it'll tell us much. We might be able to trace the origin of the pills but, again, that won't tell us exactly how Serena got them, or more to the point what, if anything, it has to do with her running away. I need to speak to her mates, and her sisters."

"She wasn't taking drugs." Fiona shook her head. "She wasn't. I would have known, and she just isn't the type."

Tanya had heard it all before.

Chapter 21

Stan Laird was friendly. A fit looking man in his early fifties, serving in the Scottish force since he had left school, he would have seen just about everything there was to see in the world of crime. Tanya had worried that there might be some resentment at what could be seen as interference, but he smiled, shook her hand, offered her coffee and seemed to genuinely understand and sympathise with her situation. It made it so much easier to take out the evidence bags and place them on his cluttered desk.

"Ah." He shook his head. "Where were they? Is it certain they were Serena's?"

"There can't be much doubt, I don't think. They were in her bedroom, hidden. Of course, my sister and her husband are in denial right now, but…"

The Scottish detective picked up the pills and envelope and handed them on to a constable for delivery to the lab. "Georgie, tell them, quick as possible will you. We've a lassie missing. Anything at all they can tell us, yes?" He turned back to Tanya. "You'll know of course that it probably won't help us to find her. It points us in the direction of the folk she might have been mixing with though. We should probably take this up a notch or two, under the circumstances. We shouldn't have missed this anyway, I'll be having a word with my lads."

He looked angry and concerned as he jotted a couple of notes on the pad in front of him. Tanya didn't envy 'his lads'.

"In fairness they were well hidden. I only found them by chance really. Anyway, look, I'm going to speak to her best friend later today, just casually at her home to start with. I thought maybe if I'm more of a 'worried auntie' than a cop she might be more open with me. I know you've talked to her already and she had nothing to tell you, but that was before this development. Is that okay? Do you want to come?"

"No, that's fine. Better if you go yourself, I think. Get back to me as soon as you can. Fill me in, will you? The more information we have the quicker we might be able to bring this wee girl home where she should be. But then you know that; I don't need to be telling you your job now, do I? I read about the angels case. That was impressive."

Tanya shook her head. "We were lucky in the end, to be honest, and we did have two women dead."

"Aye, but a fair outcome in the end."

"Yes, it was." She smiled.

They went through the investigation as much as it was. A deliberate runaway was what they had decided at first, nothing more. The quantity of drugs was so small that they agreed it might be incidental, but it did shed doubt on the image Serena's parents had painted of their 'good' girl. They talked about a television appeal but given the discovery of the pills, decided to hold off.

"I'm not sure how much good it would do," Tanya said. "My sister, well she wouldn't want to let her guard down in public, and a bit of emotion from the relatives usually plays best, don't you think?" It was a cold, hard assessment, but honest.

She drove away from the station in Fiona's car, back towards the detached houses, spacious gardens, and hidden truths.

Estella McKenzie, Serena's best friend, lived around the corner from Fiona and Graham's home. She was pretty in the way of teenaged girls from affluent families: hair shining, skin clear and her developing figure athletic and healthy. She was not quite five feet tall, hazel eyed and red haired; freckles covered her face and arms, and someone more Scottish in appearance would be hard to imagine. Estella's mother, Ruth, wondered if she should stay and Tanya assured her it was just a chat, nothing official. She hoped that this wouldn't come back to bite her later, the girl should have a responsible adult with her, but the things that Tanya wanted to talk about would be more likely to be hidden with Mum in the room.

They sat in a bright conservatory; a smooth lawn, rockery, flower borders and patio stretched away outside ending at an old stone wall. It was very gracious. The girl perched on the edge of a bamboo chair, her feet tapping on the wooden floor. She nibbled at a finger end, all her nails were chewed and the skin around them was red and sore looking. Estella kept her eyes downcast, glancing now and then towards the window but avoiding eye contact. It was textbook 'kid with something to hide'.

The courses on interview techniques were compulsory. Tanya knew the right way to handle this, she had to give the girl time, coax her gently to talk about what was on her mind, be sensitive and non-confrontational. She glanced towards the half-open door. There was no sign of Mrs McKenzie.

"There's a body in the morgue, down where I live," Tanya began. "We don't know who she is because her face has been burned off." The girl's head shot up, her eyes were wide, shocked, her hands covered her mouth. She glanced towards the hallway where her mother might be waiting; she wasn't. Tanya carried on, her voice low, no emotion, just facts.

"Somebody poured petrol on her and then threw a match on top of that. She cooked, they left her to burn away to nothing, but it didn't work, so we've got her body, black and charred, all twisted up. We don't know who did it. My team is working as hard as they can to find out, but I need to be there, I need to be doing my job with them. Now, I don't want to fart about up here looking for Serena, when there's a poor dead woman down near Oxford waiting for justice. So, why don't we just cut through the bullshit and you tell me what you know and let me get back to doing my proper job?"

The girl's eyes were swimming with tears of horror, she had hunched forward, folding herself over her knees so that when she began to speak Tanya had to lean in closer.

"She's my best mate. She said I shouldn't tell anyone. She should have been back by now, I don't know what to do." She glanced up, her eyes wide with fright.

Tanya pursed her lips. "Yes, you do know what to do, Estella. You must tell me everything. About the drugs..."

The girl gasped.

"The drugs and everything else, and don't screw me around, just give me all the information you have. Quickly, now. All of it."

Chapter 22

"She's gone to Amsterdam."

"Amsterdam!" It wasn't what Tanya had expected to hear.

"Aye, with Iain. But she made me promise not to say."

"And who the hell is Iain?"

"He's the bloke with the drugs."

"Okay, stop. Don't say another word."

Estella looked up, shaking her head in puzzlement at this change of tack.

"Mrs McKenzie, could you come in here please?"

Tanya had stepped quickly across the room and leaned out into the hallway. She heard the clatter of feet across tiles. Estella's mother poked her head around the kitchen door.

"What's wrong? I'm coming. Is she alright?"

"Yes, sorry." Tanya held up a hand in reassurance. "Yes, she's okay. It's just that what she has to tell me now is important, and it needs to be done properly, officially. I need you here as her responsible adult so that, if we need to, this can be used in evidence."

"Oh, right. Oh lord."

* * *

79

They were back in the bright garden room. Ruth McKenzie pulled another chair closer. She had taken one look at the pale, frightened face and wrapped an arm around her daughter's shoulders, tutting quietly and patting at her back. Tanya hoped that what she was about to hear wouldn't shatter any illusions she might have about her little girl. It happened too often, and it was never fun.

"I'm going to record what you say now, Estella. Do you understand that?"

The girl nodded. She had pulled a pink tissue from a box on the little table between them and was picking and shredding it between her fingers. Tanya's gut twisted when she thought of what she'd just done. If the girl referenced the case in Oxford, the shock tactics employed in getting her to talk, then Tanya was deep in the mire. She clicked the record button on her phone and set it on the tabletop, noticing in passing that there were three missed calls.

"So, you have just told me that your friend, Serena Watson, has gone to Amsterdam with Iain Laithwaite?"

"Aye." The girl answered quietly, and her mother automatically corrected the slip into dialect.

"Yes."

They both ignored her. Tanya continued, "You have also described him as 'the bloke with the drugs'. Tell me more about that?"

"I didn't take them. I've never taken them." Estella turned to her mother, shaking her head. The older woman's eyes had widened with shock. "I didn't, Mum, honestly." She turned back to Tanya, "I play hockey, it's my favourite thing, and I'm good." She turned again to her mother, "I am, aren't I? I'm good and I have to be fit, and anyway, I don't want any of that. I wouldn't ever take them."

Tanya had heard it before from panicked teens with parents sitting alongside, but in this case she thought it was probably true.

"Does Serena take drugs?"

There was a loaded silence. Tanya noticed that Charlotte McKenzie's arm had slipped from around the girl.

Eventually Estella answered, "No. Well. I think she did once. She's mad for Iain and that's why. We met him at a club we went to. She thinks he's good looking and she says she's in love with him. So, I think that was why she took the pill. She hasn't taken them since, she told me she hated it and she wouldn't."

"We found some pills in Serena's room."

Tanya was surprised to see the girl nodding her head.

"Aye. She was pretending to sell them for Iain. She took them from him and told him she'd sold them to folk, but what she did really was to pay him from out of her allowance – she has plenty of money and her mum and dad don't worry her about how she spends it." Estella glanced at her mother, even now taking the chance to make some sort of point. The girl continued, "It was just a couple now and then. She told me she'd thrown them away though."

"So, why have they gone to Amsterdam? Do you know?"

Estella shook her head. "Not really. I didn't like Iain, well, I did at first but not when I found out about the drugs. Anyway, Serena just said that she was going with him and nothing I could say would change her mind. But it was only supposed to be one day, there and back. She should have been home by now."

It was all too much, and the girl began to sob and turned to her mother who gathered her into a hug.

"Somebody will come and take a statement from you. You should have told us about this sooner, shouldn't you?"

There was an answering nod and Tanya held back her anger. She didn't want to remind the girl about how she had encouraged her to talk, not now in the middle of all this emotion.

"Do you know where he lives, this Iain?"

"No, I don't. Glasgow way I think. But I don't have his address. He's old, I bet he's about twenty, so I guess he has his own place."

"Which club did you meet him in?" When Charlotte McKenzie heard the name of the club her loud tut and stiffened body language told Tanya all she needed to know about the place.

She left the mother and daughter in the middle of a question and answer session, punctuated by tears, threats and recriminations. She went back out to the car and dialled the number for Detective Laird. With luck they might know who this Iain Laithwaite was.

She brought him up to date and left it for him to send an officer to take an official statement, and to start the investigation into the man who was now at least a suspect in selling drugs, and maybe nastier things with a young girl. As she pulled around the corner to Fiona's house she sat for a while outside in the car, listening to the quiet tick of the cooling engine and the faint rumble of traffic in the background. This wasn't going to be pretty and her palms were damp with nerves. It was so much easier with strangers. She felt for them, of course she did, but she had nothing of herself invested in their lives. With a sigh she clambered out of the car and walked towards the house where she was about to shatter forever the image of their little girl.

On the upside they knew what Serena's intentions had been and at least where she had been headed. However, something had gone wrong. One night in Amsterdam, a bit of excitement in the company of an older bloke she fancied, seemed to have stretched into something more and they had to find out pretty quickly just what that was. They had moved forward but Tanya wasn't reassured.

As she reached the door, her phone beeped, she opened the message from Charlie.

'Victim identified. Plus, witness found. Big step forward. Call me soonest.'

Chapter 23

Tanya glanced towards the glossy blue front door of her sister's house. She had to go in and tell them what she had found out. Maybe it would put some of their fears to rest, but there would be other things, new issues, to address. They would want to know everything. There would be soul-searching and discussions, there would be demands, and new anxieties. It could tie her up for hours. She looked at the phone in her hand. It was imperative to speak to Charlie. She wanted this information and would need to act on what the new developments meant for the case. Charlie was probably already on top of it and, being honest, that was one of the problems. She didn't want to lose her grip, it had to look as though she was still driving the thing. Her finger hovered over the call button. *Speak to Charlie, quickly, and then go into the house.*

The front door opened, and Fiona stepped out. She stood on the step, her arms wrapped tightly around her body, tension in every line. She took a step forward and Tanya pushed the phone back into her bag, beat back the fizz of irritation, and waved a hand towards her sister as she pushed open the car door.

"You were ages." Fiona's tone was accusatory. "I tried to phone you."

"I was in meetings; my phone was switched to silent."

"Well, what are they doing? What did you find out?"

Tanya looked at her sister. She saw the child that had made this woman: always the best, the preferred one; arrogant and entitled.

"I'll tell you in a minute, get Graham and I'll see you in the kitchen. It's under control, I've already got things moving. Right now, I need to go and talk to Charlie. I won't be long." She ignored the gasp and the affronted expression, pushed past and ran up to her room.

She didn't give Charlie a chance to speak before telling him she was in the middle of stuff and asking that he keep it as brief as possible. Tanya winced as she heard herself sounding like Fiona, but fortunately Charlie, ever the professional, didn't waste time being offended.

"We've had luck with the DNA. Our woman was on the database."

"Excellent. That's quick with the result as well."

"Yes, I put Kate onto it, she has friends in useful places it seems. Apparently, she does Triathlons with a guy from the lab. Anyway, the victim's name is Suzanne Roper. Picked up a couple of times for soliciting, known to a couple of the beat guys. Familiar story: drugs, prostitution, homeless on occasion, but recently off the streets as far as they could tell. They did think that things had improved for her lately, she had some help with detox after her last arrest and hadn't been seen around much since then. Some of the other girls had said she was doing better. We have an address for an aunt up in Yorkshire so the local lads have agreed to deliver the hard news. This came in about two hours ago and that's as far as we've got with it."

"That's brilliant, Charlie. Please pass on my thanks to Kate." The DC was a bit prickly about being overlooked due to her age and lack of progression through the ranks, but she and Tanya had formed a decent working relationship, and it was worthwhile letting her know her input had been noticed.

"Now, the witness, a bloke called Freddy Stone. I've sent you the recording of our chat, by the way. There was a knock on from that. He mentioned he'd seen someone in the alley."

"Go on."

"Well, it seems there is a regular homeless guy who hangs around down there. Colin the Cartman they call him. He's one of these with a stolen shopping trolley full of old bags and filthy duvets and what have you. The patrols are on the lookout for him now, but they had already noticed he hadn't been around since the night of the fire. Not surprising really, what with the crime scene tape and all the other activity, but I reckon he's worth looking at."

"Yes, I think we should make that a priority. Have Paul, Dan, and Sue doing a house to house," Tanya said.

"Yeah, I'm onto that, we made a start today. They are doing the pubs later. I have given them tomorrow off, it being Sunday. There won't be much happening down near the warehouse. I thought it would be more productive on Monday, not many houses there but a couple of sandwich shops, little workshops and car repair places, that sort of thing."

He'd pre-empted her again. She felt frustrated as he continued.

"How are things there?"

She couldn't criticise him, he was doing exactly what he should. She kept her voice light, positive. "I think we've had a bit of a breakthrough today. Apparently, my stupid niece was off to Amsterdam with a bloke she fancies. If Fiona had raised the alarm quicker they might have caught her at the port. We don't know where she is now. She should have been back, but of course they wouldn't be checking for her in Holland, and she would just be waved through customs at this end."

"Yeah, if she went."

"Good point, Charlie. I suppose we shouldn't assume that's what they did. Anyway, at least we have something more than we had before. They have issued a BOLF and we're checking number plate recognition to see if his car was seen heading for the ferry. Listen, tell the team 'great work' will you. Keep me informed. I need to get back there and I'm working on it."

"Yeah, it'll be good to have you back."

"Any news about your transfer?"

"Seems they've put everything on hold until this case is sorted. Bob thought it made the best sense and Merseyside were okay with it."

Another slip of the investigation away from her. She hadn't been told about this; she was sidelined. "Oh God, I'm sorry, Charlie. Is Carol okay up there with her sister?"

"I think so. We talk a few times every day. I miss 'em, but I might have a quick trip up there as soon as you're back, so hurry up, yeah."

"I'm doing my best, believe me. Everything okay at the house?"

"Yes, miss, I've cleaned the bathroom and brushed the floors." He laughed. "It's fine, Tanya, honestly. Oh, a couple of parcels arrived for you, do you want me to send them on?"

She took a moment and then said, "Tell you what, I haven't got time to deal with them right now. Could you do me a favour and send them back, ask for a refund? There should be a returns label in the packaging."

"Are you sure?"

"Yes, if you don't mind." It wouldn't make a lot of difference to her bank account, but it made her feel as if she was at least handling one of her problems.

"Okay. No probs. I'll call you tomorrow. Unless anything breaks in the meantime."

As they ended the call Tanya sighed. She was losing it, things were happening without her. This arrangement wasn't going to work for much longer. She had to finish things here and get back home. She went down to the kitchen where she could hear Fiona and Graham muttering quietly, friction hissed back and forth between them.

Chapter 24

They fell silent as Tanya came through the door. Fiona took a step forward.

"Right. What's going on? What have you found out? You could have called me. You could have kept me up to date," she said.

Tanya opened her mouth to fight back and explain that she had come immediately from her talk with Estella. She looked at her sister's face, the tightness around her eyes, the thin line of her mouth and decided to let it go. It didn't matter.

"Well, here I am now," she said, "and I do have some important news. Do you guys want to sit down?" As she said it, she saw the mistake. Her sister visibly paled; she gasped and covered her mouth with a shaking hand.

"It's okay, well no, it's not okay, but it's nothing too terrible. Look, just sit down."

"I haven't got long." Graham bit his lip as Fiona spun around on the chair seat.

She snorted and shook her head. "He has to go into the office, apparently. In the middle of all of this and my husband, Serena's father, has to go into his bloody office. On a Saturday evening as well."

Tanya looked at him, unblinking. His cheeks coloured, and he turned away, made a fuss pulling out a chair. "I won't be long. I told you I won't be long. Let's stop this and just find out what's happened. You were always a bit more understanding. You should be used to this."

Fiona snarled back, "Yes. When you were a junior doctor. Night after night on my own, weekends coping with the kids all alone. But you're supposed to be somebody now, you're supposed to be past all that."

Tanya coughed. "Okay, look you need to stop this. Just listen to me. All this other stuff can wait," she said. She then told them all that she had discovered and sat in embarrassed silence as they turned on each other again. Accusations were flung back and forth, criticism about child care decisions. Past sins were spat out and dissected. The antagonism, fear and anger ratcheted up and with it, Fiona's voice became a screech. It took Tanya back to the little terraced house when demands for the school trips that were essential to her fourteen-year-old sister, the new blazer, the better hockey stick had been demanded and financed, even though the family budget was already stretched.

It had gone on long enough. She stood up, her hands braced on the kitchen table.

"Okay, quiet both of you."

They turned to her in shock, Fiona opened her mouth to speak.

"No. Listen to me," Tanya said. "For now, you just have to let us try and find your daughter. I know this is hard, well I can imagine, but what is done is over. When she comes back you'll have to find ways to deal with all this anger and resentment. You'll have to put things right. Tonight." She raised a hand as Fiona tried again to interrupt. "Tonight, I'm going down to this club. I've got a picture on my phone of this bloke and I'm going to try and find out just where he is now. All you can do in the meantime is wait. Graham, I don't think you should go to the office. I think you should be here where we can contact you easily."

It was petty, but she took secret delight in the frustration that flicked across his face, and she knew he wouldn't argue. He didn't know she had an idea where he was really going, but in the face of her instruction it was far too difficult for him to leave now.

He wasn't giving in without a word though. "So, we just have to hang around here, waiting. Just waiting," he said.

"Unless you want to come and meet some low-lifes down at a dive in town, yes."

He struggled, a small part of him wanted to go – she knew that. He wanted to regain some of the high ground. But he was a senior doctor, a respected consultant, a member of the golf club, a Rotarian and, as his lifestyle and reputation won the battle over his chauvinism, he stormed from the room and they heard his feet thundering up the stairs, and the slam of his bedroom door.

"Who's going with you?" Fiona asked.

"Nobody."

"But that's ridiculous. They should send somebody."

"No. Look you have to try and understand. They are doing the best that they can. They have a BOLF circulated, sorry, that's 'Be on the lookout for.' And they have civilian researchers looking at CCTV of the port and checking the number plate recognition system for his car. They can't do much more. At the end of the day, Fiona, she went of her own accord. She's not underage, so, if they have had sex, that's not a crime. However, he's a dodgy bloke and we know he's involved in giving drugs to youngsters, so it would be good to get a hold of him, but that's it. I know, I do know, that for you it's the only thing that matters, getting her home, but for the local force she is one of many things that are going on. There was a bomb scare today in a shop in the town centre, a multi-vehicle crash on the road to Glasgow. An old lady was mugged and killed in her own home. These are just a few of the things I've picked up monitoring the calls. Do you see? She isn't the top of their agenda.

"Look on the bright side, we know that she chose to do this, she wasn't abducted, she wasn't in an accident. Customs at Newcastle and Hull are on high alert. They seem the most likely places, but they'll be watching everywhere else. Flights don't really make sense because there are more security checks, but the airports are aware. We are doing everything that we can under the circumstances. A lot of it is because I'm in the job, so we are getting more attention than a lot of people would."

There was no response, but Fiona's eyes swum with moisture and as she lowered her head to the table, Tanya had no choice but to wrap her arms around her sister's shaking shoulders and hold her in a way that she had rarely done before.

"I've got a picture of him sent over by DI Laird's team and I'll go down to that club and see if I can find out anything. It's the best I can do, I'm sorry, I really am but there isn't anything else unless they are picked up coming back into the country." She showed the image to her sister, but Fiona was adamant that she had never seen the man before.

"He just looks ordinary," she said. "Just like anyone you would see in the street. Okay, there's the tattoo but everyone has those these days. What is it?" Tanya enlarged the picture so that they could see more clearly the image of a bird beside his eye. "You wouldn't think he was so evil, selling drugs to children. Taking my little girl away."

"The bad guys don't have horns and tails, that's what makes the job so hard," Tanya said. She moved away, the closeness uncomfortable, and walked to the door.

"Right, I'll go and sort out something to wear, if I have anything with me. I didn't bring much." She thought of her wardrobe down in Oxford. Admittedly not many of her things were bought for going to clubs, but there would be something for certain. Then she thought of the problems that the rows of dresses and shoes, the drawers full of accessories had brought her and she was overwhelmed by a sense of sadness and dissatisfaction. She was working so bloody hard and here she was with an overdraft for the first time ever, and her sister still dictating what happened in her life, albeit inadvertently right now.

She blew out a sigh, "Why don't you make us something to eat? The club won't be busy till much later and I've had nothing much today." She turned and climbed up to her room where she took a long shower and let the hot water wash away the tears of frustration that she would never have shed in front of Fiona.

Chapter 25

It was Saturday night and the town centre was humming. It was warm for September and Tanya walked along Princes Street mingling with people emerging from the hotels and restaurants, heading for pubs and clubs – drinking and relaxing. It didn't normally bother her that she wasn't a part of that scene. Her job was what mattered. Being in the police force made her feel whole and fulfilled. Tonight though, when she knew that what she was doing was ill-advised, bordering on reckless, she felt not lonely so much as alone. It would be good to have someone with her, someone outside the family. Charlie perhaps, his quiet strength; or the bulk of Paul Harris with his off-colour comments and laddishness; the quiet sense and wiry fitness of Kate Harris. Just someone with no axe to grind.

She had told Fiona that she was acting alone, but she hadn't let Stan Laird or her team in England know. After all, she didn't really think that it would lead to much. The chances of this scum being around were very slim, life didn't work like that. But she couldn't sit in the house with her sister and brother in law. The atmosphere had already been tense, but now it was overlaid with unresolved anger and unpleasantness. She was beginning to see that things were not quite as golden in her sister's privileged life as she had been led to believe.

Anyway, even if she didn't find Iain Laithwaite, she might get a feel for the sort of people her niece had been mixing with – an idea of just how rough and debauched this place was. Estella's mother had been shocked, but she was from a different environment. There would be drugs in that world too, of that there could be little doubt, but the people who lived in the big houses wouldn't be hanging about outside seedy bars or down dark alleyways. They had no idea what that was like, so maybe this place wasn't so bad at all. Maybe it had a reputation in the wealthy suburbs that it didn't deserve.

She used the sat nav on her phone to navigate away from the view of the castle, down Frederick Street, past the Auld Hundred and towards Rose Street. When Fiona had first moved to the city these were the places you didn't go, the places where deals were done in the narrow doorways and desperate girls and women made what money they could. It had worked hard to outgrow the reputation and now the tables piled up against the windows of the closed coffee shops gave a clue as to how it would look during the day. There were upmarket shops, trendy bars, but there were also narrow streets and, away from the lights of the city, the atmosphere changed.

She walked on and was unmolested. It was still busy, people were out enjoying themselves. They weren't interested in her. Now and then a man would call out "*You alright, hen, you want some company?*" Though she felt alone, she didn't feel afraid. She might be only 160cm tall and slender but she was strong, fast and fit. She had taken all the self-defence courses, done well and enjoyed them. She worked out in the gym when she had time. She wasn't afraid of fat blokes drinking lager.

When she saw the place, she was surprised: it was worse than she had thought. Estella's mother might not have been wrong after all. She was a little shocked that the girls had dared to go through the dingy door in the dark corner of a litter-strewn square. But then, peer pressure and the need for adventure at their age had always led youngsters astray, nothing changed.

Chapter 26

She pressed down on the cold metal handle and pushed at the peeling paintwork, expecting the door to be locked. In the event, it juddered open. Behind it was a short hallway, dimly lit and smelling of old perfume and a faint whiff of cannabis. She stepped over the threshold and a voice from the corner opposite the door asked her if she was a member. She turned towards the hefty looking man sitting beside a narrow table. There was a bottle of whisky and a glass on the peeling top alongside a cash box with the lid flipped back.

"No, I'm not a member. I was supposed to meet some friends here, but I think they're late." She could have flashed her warrant card but in this sort of place, dressed as she was in her leather jacket, slim black trousers, soft white blouse, and the red spangled scarf that she had borrowed from Fiona, it would send a strange, contradictory message. Especially as she was on her own and had already lied.

"Well, it's twenty-five quid if they're not here to sign you in, but the first drink is free."

Tanya pulled her wallet from the bag she had borrowed from Fiona. Turning so that the doorman didn't get a glimpse of her police ID, she pulled out her credit card and held it up. He didn't exactly sneer, but the smile wasn't meant to be friendly and there was sarcasm in the shrug of his shoulders. He rattled the cash box on top of the desk. She was all about plastic and had no idea if there was twenty-five pounds in her wallet. She held his gaze as she unzipped the cash pocket, pulled out the notes, surprised that there were enough, peeled off three tens and dropped them onto the table.

Without turning away from her, he gathered the money into his fists and pushed them into the tin. She waited for just a few moments, the tension between them stepped up a notch and her stomach clenched, fight or flight instinct kicking in. Her hands curled into fists. But she took a breath, relaxed her shoulders. He was a Neanderthal and wanted to intimidate her, that was all.

She tipped her head to one side, raised an eyebrow and held out her hand. At last he had to look away to find a fiver. She made a mental note that if this place was as she was expecting, then she would see that the local boys would come down on it like a ton of bricks and this thug would be one of the first ones to fall. He pulled a stamp and ink pad from a drawer and held his hand out palm upwards. She ignored it and laid her hand flat on the table so that he could brand the back of it.

"Just in case you have to go out looking for your 'friends'," he said with a grin.

She realised with a sick turn of her stomach that he had pegged her as a prostitute, or at the least a girl on the make. It was the obvious lie about friends, of course. She turned away without another word. It didn't matter, it was in her hands to get back at him. As she thought of him cuffed and pushed into the back of a squad car she grinned. First, she had to find the thing to make that happen, but even if there was nothing connected with Serena's disappearance, she would find something. It would make the trip worthwhile, just to bring the door thug down to earth.

She wasn't undercover – she had done the course. You didn't go undercover on your own. You had briefings and permission and tons of back up, you had a plan and probably a wire, and somewhere you had your gas canister. She looked at the tiny leather bag, no room for more than her phone and wallet. She hadn't even put in a tin of hairspray or deodorant which could, in an emergency, blind someone for enough time to kick them in the groin and run away.

She would say she wanted to get a feel for the sort of place her niece had been, so that she could help her sister with child care decisions. But, if she found enough evidence to bring in the heavy mob, then the reasons for being there would be for appearance's sake, to make sure there was nothing to jeopardise a case. She was just an off-duty cop, having a night out and trying to help her family.

Chapter 27

It was still early, just after eleven, and the dim room was almost empty. There were musicians on a tiny stage opposite the bar, which was the source of most of the light.

The band was still setting up. Harsh electronic noises, as they plugged in equipment, were met with jeers from the few customers. Some were well down on their drinks. A couple of men stood alone at the bar, and further along a small group gathered around two girls who were perched on high bar stools, giggling and canoodling with the men. Pecks on the cheek or longer, deeper smooches, hands stroking at the backs of necks, thighs, and in one case a quick grope of an almost naked breast which resulted in a slap and a laugh. Tanya felt overdressed, too formal for the surroundings in which she was trying to avoid being noticed. She pulled off her jacket and draped it over the back of her tall chair, she pushed the sequinned scarf into her pocket, and undid the top button on her blouse.

"Alright, hen?" The barman was young, long-haired and greasy looking. He had already picked up a white wine glass, making an assumption that got Tanya's back up.

She looked at the glass, and glanced at him.

"A pint of Guinness, please?"

He shook his head. "We don't serve pints."

He put down the glass and waited.

"In that case, I'll have a dry Martini please, with an olive."

She hated Martinis, loathed olives, but he wasn't going to intimidate her.

He moved away and dragged out a bottle, a glass, and a dish with some grim looking liquid in the bottom and three olives swilling back and forth. To give him credit he polished the glass and rimmed it with salt, there was even a fancy plastic stick with a saltire at one end and the olive at the other. She showed him the stamp on the back of her hand, he placed a paper coaster on the bar and the drink on top. She had little experience of clubs, her drinking was done in the pub or at home, but this was not at the high end. She supposed the very sleaziness was attractive to girls like Serena and Estella, so different from the clean, bright world they inhabited. She had no intention of trying the Martini, but she wrapped her fingers around the stem of glass and swivelled it back and forth.

Listening to the increasing swirl of noise, Tanya suddenly felt a little foolish. She wasn't sure why she was here, wasn't there something more productive she should be doing? There was the video of the interview with the witness that she hadn't had a chance to watch. She could go over the daily reports Charlie had sent on. She glanced down at the drink in front of her. Much of the salt had fallen off and the small paper coaster was crinkled and disintegrating. This was sad and sordid and pointless.

She reviewed the last couple of days. She had done some good, cleared up part of the mystery. The locals were on it now with a direction for their enquiries. There wasn't much more for her to contribute. It would be more sensible to head back to Oxford. Things at Fiona's were very unpleasant, and they might be better able to sort things out without her there. She wasn't going to spill the beans on Graham, it was nothing to do with her. Okay, he was a cheating swine, but it wasn't any of her business. She could keep in touch with Fiona by phone or better still email. Surely, she had shown enough sisterly support and could have her life back.

She would go home. Tomorrow.

A noisy group surged through the door, four men and three girls. The girls were a mix of bare skin and bling and they were all at a boisterous stage of drunkenness. They swarmed up to the bar and demanded champagne. There was a fuss while the cork was popped, the fizz poured, and then an ice bucket plonked onto the bar, condensation dribbling down the sides. The group leader – there was always one, self-appointed - leaned across the bar. He spoke quietly to the barman who glanced around the room and shook his head. Money changed hands, there was a short conversation and then they separated. The notes didn't go into the till, but into the barman's pocket.

A few more customers drifted in and Tanya watched them all. The bloke behind the counter kept things going, and now he had help from a tubby girl in a tight pink top and a stretchy miniskirt. The noise level was increasing, it was hot and stuffy. A lone man at the far end of the bar had been staring at her, blatantly; he'd smiled and nodded. She didn't want to deal with him, she didn't want to deal with anyone. She wanted to be in her own home, clean, and in bed with her laptop. This was a mistake.

Tanya pulled her coat from the back of the chair. She began to slide to the edge of the seat. That was when she saw him. He leaned across the bar towards the barman who served him with a lager and a double whisky chaser. They leaned together whispering and the barman nodded in the direction of the champagne group. A small package changed hands. It was palmed quickly, and there was the roll of notes coming back the other way. Damn! She should have been recording: she'd missed her chance to make some sort of sense of this wasted evening. She pulled her phone out, made a pantomime of pretending to text as she recorded the two men. She swung around as if searching the growing crowd, her phone held low, discreetly recording the barman moving down the narrow space in front of the bottles and glasses. He gestured to the noisy group, and in moments they were grinning and high fiving each other, slipping the pills between their lips. She had proof that drugs were changing hands. It wasn't much but it was something.

She regained her seat and aimed the camera at the newcomer. His hands were on the bar top, long fingers drumming on the wet surface. He was slightly less than average height. His hair was thick and wavy, it was long enough to fall forward as he leaned down and then he swept it back revealing the glint of an earring and something on the side of his face, just below his eye. The tiny bird tattoo was only visible because he was leaning into the brighter lights behind the bar, watching the champagne group with a grin twisting his thin lips. She watched him for a moment, still recording – she wanted a better view on the phone. She continued her pretence of texting, tutted and glanced at her watch. He looked towards her and she knew without a doubt. Iain Laithwaite was less than a metre away. She slid to her feet and walked around and on towards the ladies. She peered around the room, filled appreciably by now, but nowhere could she see her niece.

She didn't pause but walked on and through into the toilets. It wasn't bad, still reasonably clean, smelling of chemical air freshener. Bright lights were harsh and unforgiving on her pale face. She brushed her hair, used the lavatory and checked the picture that Stan Laird had sent. There was no doubt about who it was outside in the bar, so, in that case, where was Serena?

Chapter 28

She had to get back out there before he had a chance to leave. Tanya reached for the door handle as it swung inwards and the barmaid scuttled in. They smiled at each other and the girl went to the washbasins and leaned into the mirror. She began to tidy her eye makeup and fluff her long hair.

Tanya moved across. "Excuse me, you work behind the bar, don't you?"

"Aye."

"Look, I was supposed to meet my niece here and she hasn't shown up." It was a fractured version of the truth, but as she clicked on the image that she had of Serena, the young woman leaned over to peer at the screen.

"Oh aye, I ken that lassie. One of the posh girls, slumming it. It's not my business but if she was my niece I'd tell her to find somewhere better than this to spend her time."

"Yes. I know what you mean. I haven't been in here before. I was surprised that she liked it. You haven't seen her tonight, have you?"

The girl shook her head and turned back to the mirror. "No, not for a couple of weeks. You should meet her outside, take her off somewhere nice. That's what I'd do."

"Yes. I think I will. Thanks so much."

"No bother, hen. See ya." And with that she disappeared into the cubicle and closed the door.

Tanya went back into the bar where Iain Laithwaite was drinking a second half of lager, his whisky lined up alongside. She turned and slipped through the swinging door out into the gloomy corridor.

The bulky doorman looked up at her. "Your friends not turned up then?"

She wondered if she should ask him about Serena, but he was streetwise, not as naïve as the barmaid, and he would suss her out in moments. She shook her head. "I'm going to meet them outside, we're going somewhere else."

"Expensive visit for you then." He grinned at her.

"Oh, well worth it, honestly." And with the cryptic comment she left him frowning after her as the door slammed shut behind her.

Chapter 29

Tanya crossed the road and found a recessed shop doorway from where she had a decent view of the club entrance. She knew that it could be a long wait so she zipped up her jacket and thrust her hands deep into the pockets. It wasn't too cold, but it was September in Edinburgh after all. She felt the scratch of the sequins on the scarf that Fiona had loaned her, took it out and wrapped it around her neck.

There weren't many people around, and those that were, either wobbled along the road hanging on to drunken friends, or scuttled past towards last buses or the comfort of their hotel rooms.

This is what she did; this is what being a copper was about. She had a bad guy to follow and she felt the misery of the last hour slide away.

It would be sensible to let someone know, but whom? If she contacted Stan Laird, he would tell her to go home and leave it to them to sort it. But she was committed now and didn't want to beg for a part in whatever was going to happen. If she called Charlie, he could do nothing to help her from the middle of England and would tell her to call for back up. Again, the most likely result would be having it taken out of her hands.

It was the sensible thing, but this bloke had caused her no end of grief and she wanted him for herself. She also wanted her niece home as soon as possible; this whole mess over and done. Following him now was the right thing to do. It was gut feeling but she had relied on it before and been right. She would follow him, see where he was staying and then call for help to take him in and pick up Serena. It was fine.

If he was in a car, that would make the decision for her. Fiona's car was parked in the multi-storey in Castle Terrace. There was not a snowball's chance in hell that he was parked there as well. Somewhere in the back of her mind there had been the vague hope that if she had found the couple at the club, she could bring Serena away with her and leave the rest of it to Stan Laird and his men. Stupid when she thought about it now – badly planned. This whole thing had been done to get a feel for the place, on the off chance that she could speak to someone who knew him or Serena, or maybe knew where he lived. That hadn't worked – the barmaid had only confirmed what they already knew. She pushed the thoughts aside to concentrate on the job at hand. This result was more than she could have hoped for and at the rate he was drinking she didn't think he could be driving, so it could still work out.

He emerged, alone, after about a half an hour. That wasn't too bad, she hadn't become too cold, though it would be good to be moving. He glanced back and forth before turning right and heading towards the city centre. He swaggered along the middle of the pavement, glancing casually at shop windows, stepping around empty fast food cartons, and the occasional beer can. Tanya stayed on her own side of the road, keeping to the shadows, cursing the leather heels on her shoes for the noise they made. The streets were well lit, and it was easy to keep him in sight.

Almost inevitably it had begun to rain: fine, soaking drizzle that brought with it a cold promise of winter. She turned up her collar and kept on.

They walked for ten minutes or so, and then he slowed, glanced from side to side and turned to look behind him. He lifted his arm to look at his watch, and wiped rain from his face with the palm of his hand. He shook his head, pushing fingers through his hair. With a sideways step he entered the dark maw of an alleyway.

Tanya drew into another doorway, this one the entrance to a small block of flats. She could see the shade of him, leaning against the wall, and then the flare of small flame and the red glow of a cigarette. She heard footsteps heading towards her and flattened against the damp wall of her hiding place. The newcomer paused a moment at the pavement edge before crossing towards the passage where Iain waited. She could tell only that it was probably a man. He was dressed in dark clothes, his shoulders hunched against the rain. He raised a hand towards the figure in the alley who did not respond, except to throw down the half-smoked cigarette. He ground the stub under his foot, coughed and spat onto the pavement before moving further into the darkness.

There was no point trying to record this, it would need special equipment to get any sort of useable footage, and she was too far away. She slipped from the doorway and sidled into the next entrance from where she could see the two men more clearly. They shook hands, a strange courtesy under the circumstances, and there was a short conversation. Goods changed hands and the second man moved away, walking quickly. He soon disappeared around a corner. Laithwaite watched him go and then turned to the wall and urinated against the dirty stone. Subconsciously she screwed up her nose as, zipping his flies, he moved back into the street, turned to face the way that he had come and headed in the direction of the club.

If he had simply been collecting more drugs and was now heading back to offload them, Tanya knew she could be in for a longer, colder, wetter wait. It had to be done though, and when she judged it safe she stepped out of the shadows.

Chapter 30

Iain Laithwaite turned before they reached the club, and headed towards Princes Street and along by the station. He was walking with purpose now, no longer distracted by the shops and closed cafes. Pulling up the collar on his coat he began to stride out more quickly. He gave all the appearance of a man going home. Tanya felt a rising sense of excitement.

They were away from the stylish shops and hotels and onto a road of small newsagents, food shops, offices and stationery outlets. There were flats above many of the retail spaces and narrow passages between the buildings. It was an area of dark, damp corners and ill-lit road junctions. There was nobody about, except once or twice she saw a rough sleeper filling a doorway, the dark hump of a sleeping bag dampening in the drizzle. Tanya was very aware that she was alone, and no one knew where she was, or what she was doing. But she couldn't give up because she was convinced he was leading her to Serena. Once she found where the girl was, then she would call for help and stand by while the local force cleaned up this mess.

Water dripped into her eyes and she brushed it aside with a cold hand. Her trousers were soaked, and the rain ran down her leather coat and dripped against the back of her legs. It was dark and uncomfortable, and she was in her element, thrilled and focused.

He slowed eventually beside a small shop. She was on the other side of the road and could see clearly as he unlocked the door and stepped into a dark hallway. Lights flicked on, shining through the skylight above the door and pooling on the wet pavement. The building had two upper floors. The top was in darkness, but in the right-hand room of the first floor, a light showed dimly through curtains hanging limply at an old sash window.

It wasn't long before she saw a shadow move across the thin fabric. It was him. She could tell by his size and the set of the narrow shoulders. He stood for a moment, silhouetted in the creamy glow, and then moved away into the room.

Tanya crossed the narrow road. There were three bell pushes beside the front door. Although there were tiny windows for the insertion of a name card nobody had bothered, though in the bottom one someone had pushed in a piece of paper with 'garden flat' scrawled across in blue ink.

She walked past the shop window and turned down the alley at the side. It was littered and running with water, several empty cat food tins clattered under her feet and she cursed as she slid them away with the side of her shoe. Where the old stone ended there was a wooden fence. She grabbed the top, and using her feet for purchase, pulled up high enough to peer over. Calling it a garden had been an exaggeration but there was a small space with a couple of flower pots and an old metal garden table. The ground floor was dark and silent.

She walked further along the alley to the corner and then turned to follow the line of the fence to the gate. It had an old-fashioned handle with a thumb push to operate the latch. She wrapped her fingers around it and pressed down on the flat metal disk. Though the latch operated smoothly, when she pushed at the gate it refused to open. She pushed against it again. It was caught at the top and she stretched up on her toes, worming her fingers over the splintered wood and feeling for the bolt which she knew must be there. She felt the metal but could barely reach it with her fingertips. She turned away and crept back and forth in the alley searching for something to stand on. A dog barked in another yard and she stopped and waited until it quieted.

Puddles of gritty, grimy water splashed up onto her legs and into her shoes. The rain was a full-on torrent by now and water was beginning to run down the gutter in the middle of the alley. Tanya's hair hung in dripping rat's tails around her face and she gathered it in one hand, twisted it and tucked it inside her jacket collar. It soaked her blouse through to the skin, and she shivered, shrugged her shoulders and carried on. She had walked away from the place where the dog had alarmed, pushing at a couple more gates as she went. They were all locked.

What she ought to do now was to call for help. She had found the man they were looking for and he was, presumably, inside for the next few hours. She pulled out her mobile phone. There was no signal here between the tall houses because it was effectively a valley surrounded by stone walls. She would need to go back to the main road.

There were lights at a junction beyond the passage so she walked straight on towards it. Near the bottom, beside a dilapidated gate, was a small pile of discarded rubbish. There were a couple of crates that were rotted and crumbling and of no use, but there was a plastic box without a lid. She flipped it over and climbed carefully onto the top, holding onto the fence for support and to spread some of her weight. It bulged inward, but she didn't hear a crack of plastic. She eased her hand from the fence and slid her feet towards the edges, where the plastic might be stronger. She gave a little bounce and it didn't break. She grinned and hissed out a quiet "Yes".

Back at the gate the extra height allowed her to reach the bolt. She expected a padlock, but when she grabbed the hasp it pulled upwards and slid smoothly down the groove in the lock.

Once inside the garden she turned and relocked the gate. It was second nature to close off means of escape in case Laithwaite made a run for it. She checked her phone again wondering if it might have picked up a signal now she was out of the narrow alley. It hadn't, so she moved down the garden to where the ground floor flat had a single-story extension with a glazed door, and a corrugated metal roof.

Light shone from the rear window of the first floor flat, diffused by a net curtain. All thought of calling for help was forgotten now that she saw the chance to peer inside.

She picked up the metal garden table and carried it with her. It was as easy as mounting a flight of stairs to clamber up and stand on the edge of the building. She tested the strength of the roof. When it held she moved slowly forward, heel and toe across the inner edge, supporting herself with a hand on the wall until she was able to grasp the ledge. Two more steps were all it took, and she was beneath the window. She could hear the voices of the people inside. One was harsh and impatient she judged it to be Laithwaite, and another, quieter. There was the slam of a door, then silence.

Chapter 31

Tanya steadied herself on the slick metal of the roof. Clinging to the spalling window ledge, she pulled herself up to squint through gaps in the lace curtain.

There was a single ceiling light covered with an old-fashioned shade illuminating the small room. The corners were shadowed and dim. On the sofa, in front of a two-bar electric fire, she could see the hunched shape of Serena. The girl was resting her chin on her hands and staring at the dull, grey carpet. She raised a finger and brushed at her eyes. Tanya was swept with a flood of pity. The girl was young and naïve and yes, stupid, but she looked so forlorn sitting in the nasty little room dressed in her designer hoody and her expensive trainers. Her long, auburn hair was lank and greasy and tied back in a loose ponytail. She didn't appear to be hurt, but some damage wouldn't be so easily visible; the truth remained to be seen.

Tanya tapped lightly on the glass and scratched a fingernail down the pane. There was no response and so she knocked a little louder. She had to do this without bringing Iain Laithwaite back from wherever he was.

Still Serena hadn't heard her, she rapped with the ring that she wore on her right hand and the girl looked up.

Tanya knocked again. Serena leaned forward to peer towards the window. She glanced backwards at the door and then in one rapid movement, stood from the couch and dashed across the room.

Tanya waved upwards with her hand, but Serena didn't need instruction. She was already pulling at the sash window, tugging at the awkward little handles – her face twisted with effort.

They managed to force it open millimetre by millimetre. As soon as there was space, Tanya wormed her way through to land in a heap on the floor. Serena bent and helped her to stand, panic rounding her eyes as she grabbed at Tanya's shoulders.

"Quick, quick, if he comes in, he'll be furious! Take me home."

"Are you hurt?"

Although Serena shook her head, the tears that flooded her eyes told a different story, and Tanya gathered her close and held her for a moment and let her cry. "It's all right, it's okay. I'm taking you home and you'll be fine."

"I thought he was lovely, Aunty Tan. I'm such an idiot." Her niece had reverted to the childhood name and Tanya felt sad there had been so very few times she had heard it, and not at all for a long time now.

"I know, I know. We'll talk about it all later. Let's just get you home. Your mum and dad are frantic."

Serena wiped at her nose and her eyes with the sleeve of the hoody.

"I bet Mum's been mad though, hasn't she? I bet she's furious with me, she'll hate me now, and Daddy..."

The tears came heavier now. "I thought I knew why we were going to Holland. I thought we were going to get some weed, some pills, but it wasn't that." She was unable to continue, and Tanya saw the haunted, damaged look crawl into her eyes. It would never really leave, not completely, no matter how much therapy her sister's money bought, and how strong this girl turned out to be.

Now was not the time to open the floodgates, but Serena was still talking.

"I don't remember all that happened, there were pills and there were men and…" The next sentence was too difficult, she let it go. She paused, shook her head before continuing.

"He wasn't going to bring me back. He was sneaking away. I was pretending to be out of it, so they'd leave me alone, but I saw him, I ran after him. He was going to leave me there with no money, nothing, leave me with those men. We were out in the street and I was crying, screaming really; people were looking, it was horrible."

"I know, love, I know. But tell me later. You can tell us everything later."

Still the girl was babbling, tears rolling unchecked down her cheeks and she was sniffing and gulping. Tanya tried again to shepherd her towards the window.

"He made me come here. He said if I ran away he'd find me, said he knew where I lived, where I went to college, and he does. I can't get away from him. He said I was the biggest mistake he'd ever made. I've been such an idiot and I've been so scared."

Tanya didn't think the girl had any idea how lucky she was to be still alive. They would get the full story eventually, but how she had not been killed and thrown into a Dutch canal it was difficult to understand. Maybe it had been just a step too far for Laithwaite. She tried again to move them both towards the window.

"Come on, I'll help you down, it's easy and then I'll call for help. We can sort everything out, once you're safe. You can tell us everything, we'll get you help, you'll be okay."

But it was too late, she had known it had taken too long, that they'd made too much noise. The door flung back on its hinges crashing into the wall, a shower of plaster cascading onto the carpet. Iain Laithwaite stood in the doorway armed with a nasty looking knife. The handle was fluorescent green, the blade serrated down one edge.

It was long with an upturned end. Serena whimpered when she saw him and stepped behind Tanya who had thrown out an arm to push her backwards.

She held up a hand and took a pace towards him.

"Put that down, Iain. Don't let's be stupid. We can sort all this out, but that's just making things worse." She took another step and he came to meet her.

Chapter 32

Iain Laithwaite braced himself, legs apart, bent a little at the knees. He brandished the knife in front of him, waved it back and forth. He was wiry, young, and it was an evil knife.

They were bad odds, and Tanya tried again to talk to him. "Calm down. There's no sense to this. Back up is coming, you might as well give it up."

"Who the hell are you?"

"Detective Inspector Tanya Miller seconded to the local force." It was a lie, but it didn't matter if it helped to intimidate him. It didn't.

"What the hell are you doing here. You've broken in. You'd better have a warrant."

He was clutching at straws and she allowed a smile to spread across her face.

"Nice try, Iain. I don't need a warrant. Not when I believe someone is at risk and Serena here, well let's be honest, she is definitely at risk. You need to just give it up now. You don't want this to get any worse and attacking me is going to bring down a whole world of hurt."

She had edged forward as she spoke, every nerve alive, her muscles tensed. He glanced at Serena who was cowering beneath the window.

"What's she told you? She's been lying. She wanted to come with me, wanted to party and then when it got going, she panicked," he said.

"No, I don't think so," Tanya said, "but look, come and tell your side of it. Maybe there has been a misunderstanding." There was a gasp from behind her, but she didn't turn, didn't react.

"No, Aunty Tan, no. It's true, I didn't know what he was going to do. I didn't know what would happen."

"Aunty Tan?" he raised an eyebrow. "Aunty. Ha! So not a copper after all."

The useless little bag was still slung across her body and Tanya lifted it from where it dangled next to her hip. "I'll show you my warrant card."

She grasped the strap and pulled it over her head; another half step forward hidden by the movement. She lowered a hand towards the zip. His eyes flicked downward. She struck. With all the strength of her shoulders, she swung the bag in a wide arc towards him. He had a strong grip on the weapon, and though the bag knocked it sideways, and the handle wrapped around it, he hung on. She still had one end tight in her hand and tugged hard, unbalancing him. He stumbled a little, shook the arm holding the knife, and pulled at the bag with his other hand. He was distracted by his attempts at untangling the mess and Tanya stepped forward, bringing up her knee towards his groin. If she had hit home it would have done the job, but he turned away enough to protect his balls and she connected with his inner thigh. It made him gasp with pain but didn't make him the roiling mess on the floor she hoped for.

He still battled with the knife, trying to loosen the straps caught in the deep serrations on the wicked blade. Tanya threw herself towards him, aiming to knock him off his feet but again luck was on his side, and though he staggered backwards, the wall broke his fall. The bag had done all it could and slid to the floor uselessly as Iain Laithwaite grinned, the knife back in his full possession.

Tanya turned at an angle and charged, leading with the elbow, connecting with his throat. She felt him go slack as he choked out a gurgle. His eyes clouded briefly, and she thought she had him. He was made of tough stuff though and the arm holding the knife sliced upwards ripping through the leather of her jacket and she felt the flood of warm liquid that told her she was cut. She would lose it now if she didn't take him in the next seconds. Her hands darting under the blade she grabbed at his wrist, twisted it upwards and backwards, it wasn't textbook, but as near as she could manage. What she lost in technique she made up for with brute force.

She felt the crunch of bone, and heard him scream. The blade hit the wall and fell to the floor. Hands locked together now behind his neck, she dragged him forward towards her knee which she brought up with all her energy. There was the crunch of gristle and spatter of blood and as he sagged in her arms she knew the fight was hers.

Chapter 33

Tanya threw her phone to Serena. "See if there's a signal."

"Yes, it's okay," Serena said.

"Great, now find Stan Laird on there, tell him who you are, tell him quickly what's happened and say we need an ambulance." While that was done Tanya spent the time rolling an unconscious Iain Laithwaite into the recovery position and watching to make sure he didn't choke on his tongue or the blood from his broken nose. She had kicked the knife well into the corner out of harm's way. Just in case.

By the time the troops arrived, he was conscious but groggy, lying on the carpet groaning and swearing but no longer any threat to anyone. They laid him on a backboard, his neck in a collar, an infusion plugged into his arm. The first responder had called for a second ambulance to take Tanya to A & E to have the horrible gash in her arm, currently wrapped in a sparkly red scarf, attended to. They had a struggle with Serena, she begged to be allowed to just go home. Everyone agreed that going from the current situation straight into another, which would be just as tense and emotional, was never going to be the right thing for someone in her fragile mental state. She cried and pleaded but eventually they persuaded her to go with her aunt and called for an ecstatic Fiona and Graham to meet them at the hospital.

Alone in the tiny A & E cubicle, Tanya began to go over what would be required next. A report to Stan Laird. A conversation with her sister, which was going to be ghastly, and of course official questions about her role in all that had happened. That would be protracted, there would be an inquiry, a man had been hurt and she had been injured. It was going to generate a mountain of paperwork, interviews and statements, but there would be no getting away from it. She relived the events of the last hours. She had no choice but to protect herself and Serena. He was armed, he was dangerous, and she had told him who she was. She had not had clear grounds to arrest him, but she had identified herself. She didn't think she had done anything wrong, except perhaps not calling for backup, but these days cunning lawyers could pick and pick at something until it unravelled.

Suddenly, she found that she just didn't care very much. She had found her niece. It had been too late to save her from harm, but the harm had already been done well before Tanya became involved. She couldn't imagine that there would be any sort of censure regarding her fight with Iain Laithwaite, and if there was, she would deal with it. Right now, all she wanted was to be on her own at home. She lay her head back on the hospital pillow and closed her eyes.

Her phone was in the bag on the chair beside her narrow bed, and although it was on silent, she clearly heard it buzzing. She rolled over until she could reach with her good arm and hoisted the whole thing on to her belly. By the time she found the phone and dragged it out the ringing had stopped. Charlie's number was at the top of the missed calls list. Before she had a chance to phone him back, the message icon popped up.

'We need a Skype conference tomorrow. We need you back here. Can you give me an update? Bob Scunthorpe is getting twitchy, he wants things to move more quickly. Hope things are going okay there – Charlie.'

She responded with a short text: 'Things here have come to a head. Should be back tomorrow or Monday. Serena is safe.' It was enough, she could give him all the gory details when she saw him. She knew that tomorrow, Sunday, would be almost impossible, but she was going to try.

A nurse pushed through the curtain at the entrance to the cubicle. With a tut and a shake of her head, she grabbed the phone, pushed it into the bag and placed the whole lot out of the way on the floor. She pulled a steel trolley from the corner.

"Right, doctor's on his way, we need to put some stitches in that arm and get you some painkillers and probably antibiotics. Are your tetanus jabs up to date?" the nurse said.

"Yes, I think so."

"Excellent, well lay back and relax, this won't take long and it shouldn't be too uncomfortable."

The nurse had lied, it hurt like the devil and they told her there was damage to the tendons and muscles. Probably not enough to need surgery but she may need physio before she regained full strength and movement.

"How's my niece?" Tanya asked, mostly to take her mind off what the baby-faced doctor was doing to her arm because she didn't think they'd tell her much.

"The poor thing," the nurse said. "Her mum's with her now and the doctor's seen her. I can't tell you much more than that, but it's going to be a long hard road for her if what we have heard is true. But she's young, God willing she'll find a way."

Tanya didn't believe in a benevolent deity but right then she sort of hoped that there was some divine help for her niece because her life had changed irrevocably and she was in need of serious support.

Chapter 34

They would not let Tanya see Serena because the girl had been sedated. They had given her a morning-after pill, taken swabs and blood samples, she would be screened for STDs, HIV, and hepatitis. Fiona had sobbed and wiped constantly at her bloodshot eyes as she went through the indignities and discomforts her daughter had suffered at the hands of the medics.

They were sitting together on hard plastic chairs in the reception area, waiting for Graham to bring the car from the parking space.

"She wouldn't see her dad. She said she was too embarrassed. It broke him in pieces," Fiona said.

Though Tanya knew a bit more about her brother-in-law than she really wanted, she did feel for him. It was a common enough reaction with the young girls she had dealt with who had been sexually abused. It would take a long time for them all to recover. They would never be quite the same again.

"I want him in jail, the swine. I want him in jail, and the others – all of them." There was a slight edge of hysteria to Fiona's voice and Tanya didn't think this was the time to explain that actually, there was very little likelihood of that happening. He might be sentenced for his attack on a police officer, that remained to be seen; and there were the drugs, but that was minor in the great play of things.

For the rest of it; it had happened in a foreign country, Serena had gone with him knowingly and had even understood that they were probably going to smuggle drugs. She had no clear knowledge of what had happened because of what she said they had given her. It was a nasty mess all round. She was not underage and couldn't prove that Iain Laithwaite or anyone else had raped her. She had some physical signs of rough sex, but they were healing already. It did seem he had locked her up against her will but in all of it the girl was not completely innocent. A defence lawyer would tear her to pieces even if the Procurator Fiscal thought there was enough to progress with it. In the end the result would probably not be worth the trauma. It was unfair, a young girl had been taken advantage of, a family changed forever, but it was an old story and they would have to find a way through, most probably without the justice they wanted.

Tanya looked at her distraught sister and simply shook her head. She couldn't face the arguments, the demands, the harassment, the heartbreak, if she tried to explain. She would leave it to other people, Stan Laird maybe, or the solicitors they had already contacted. It was cowardly, but she'd had enough and there was nothing that she could do to change any of it, no matter how much Fiona railed and cried.

The doctor had prescribed strong painkillers, but Tanya had pushed the little box into her pocket unopened. She wanted to tie up as many of the loose ends as she could while adrenaline still surged through her bloodstream. When the withdrawal hit she knew she would be poleaxed and the plan was to have that happen on the train on the way home. She needed to hit the ground running when she got back to Oxford. When the report for Stan Laird was written, she would go over all the emails from Charlie and finally watch the interview with their only witness. She had no intention of sleeping. Red Bull and coffee were what she needed, not painkillers.

Chapter 35

Growing up in a home with such an imbalance between the two of them, Fiona and Tanya had argued often. Recent years had been peaceful but mainly because they were rarely in contact. When Tanya walked down the stairs on Sunday morning, her bags packed, and asked if she could have a lift to the station Fiona exploded.

"Where the hell do you think you're going?" she said.

Tanya had expected this and was determined to keep things as calm as possible. She was exhausted, she had spent most of the night filling in the forms that Stan Laird had forwarded on for her, then reviewing her own case. As soon as she judged it a reasonable hour of the morning, she had sent emails, and asked questions, disturbing Charlie, Stan Laird, and even the Fire Officer at home. Finally, she had phoned the hospital to check on Iain Laithwaite. He was due to be discharged later with his broken nose and damaged wrist; neither of which caused her a moment's guilt. She had booked her ticket, checked her bank account – the sight of which depressed her – and now this.

"I'm going home. I'm done here." Her eyes felt filled with sand and every part of her ached. She had her pills in her pocket and as soon as she sat down on the train she would take them and sleep away all the journey. Charlie was meeting her, and they would go directly to headquarters so that she could look at the noticeboards and add her own notes to those already there.

Fiona was standing too close, invading Tanya's personal space, filling the air between them with fury and coffee breath.

"Don't be so bloody ridiculous. You can't go home," she said.

Tanya closed her eyes and sighed. "I'll be back in a little while. I will more than likely have to come up to address the inquiry, though Detective Inspector Laird said he'll do his best to avoid it. Maybe we can Skype it or something. Anyway, that's not today and I really do need to get back. I have an ongoing case, Fiona, you know this." She put her bag on the floor and reached out to lay a hand on her sister's arm.

Fiona stepped back, eyes blazing. "What about us? What about me and Serena, what about your family?

"There's nothing else for me to do. You've arranged a lawyer, you've organised somewhere for Serena to go to get the care she needs. There's nothing more that I can do. Really, Fiona, think about it."

"You should be here, you should be supporting me. Bloody Graham's gone off first thing this morning, I have no idea where he is, and now you're buggering off. Does nobody care about what I've just gone through?"

"Of course we care. I care." In all honesty, she had to wonder how much Graham did care, leaving his wife this morning. She had no proof that he was seeing another woman in the midst of this crisis but surely if he had gone anywhere else he would have been open about it.

"No, no, you can't go, I won't let you." Shaking her head Fiona stepped backwards down the hall and leaned against the front door, her arms folded across her chest.

"Fiona, you don't need me. Half the time you don't even like me. You've got all the support you need. Someone will be coming later today from the local force to talk to you, they'll help you with the legal stuff. You've got your own kids, you've got Serena who needs you. There is no reason for me to be here now. I found her. For God's sake what more do you want from me?"

The final statement was the result of pain, tiredness and frustration. She saw the hurt in her sister's eyes, but in that moment acknowledged that she didn't have any real depth of feeling for this woman. Serena was different, she was young and vulnerable and had to be found. But Fiona was demanding and selfish, had been since childhood, and Tanya acknowledged a truth that she had always known. It had been subdued because of guilt, upbringing and expectations, but she didn't like her sister. Not at all.

"Well, I'm not taking you to the station. I'm just not." Still standing guard on the door, Fiona lifted her chin and stared at Tanya with cold, hard eyes.

"Okay, suit yourself. Tell Serena I hope she's better soon and if she ever wants to talk to me, she knows my number." Stamping through the kitchen and down the drive, Tanya brushed away tears. She didn't know where they came from; anger, the need for sleep, or just a strange sort of loneliness, because she had just left what little family she had and didn't think she would ever want to see them again.

Chapter 36

Rain soaked his shoulders. He'd known a time when he'd cursed the sunshine and the heat. That was when he had a wife and a little girl waiting for him at home. Back when he didn't jump at shadows and the sound of fireworks didn't turn him into a snivelling wreck. Back when his life made some sort of sense, even if he was miles away sitting on a hill watching goats and scruffy kids running between concrete block houses.

There were some buildings nearby, boat houses, he could shelter there. But then the man might think he hadn't come. Might just drive away. Wait by the bridge he'd said. There were rivercraft moored nearby – power boats and a couple of barges – all dark and quiet. Nobody here now in this rain. That was good, nobody to see him. He hated being seen, hated being pointed at, pitied, scorned, it wasn't fair. None of it was fair.

After today he might buy a waterproof. A cheap one. The money was for Leanne, but maybe just a couple of pounds could buy a jacket and some new trainers from the market.

He should have made the bloke meet him in town. He'd become weak, maybe he'd always been weak and only wearing the uniform made him strong. Well, that was gone now; that and everything else.

Oh, did it matter? As long as he brought the money, that was the thing. Then he'd leave, he wasn't going to bleed the bloke dry. Just this one payment, something to send to his ex for Leanne's birthday, then he'd go back for his stuff and head off, or perhaps he wouldn't go back. He didn't need the stuff, he had lost track now of why he'd begun to collect it. He stuck his hand in his pocket and pulled out the picture of himself with Leanne when she was five, just starting school. He had that, he didn't need the rest of it. He could just keep on walking.

He saw now that he had no choice. This bloke would always be around. Even if he moved away from the church and the car park, the man would be in the town. There would always be a risk. This had been a bad idea, this had put him in danger. Could it put Leanne in danger? The bloke didn't know about her, did he? Suzanne had known, she could have told him when she met him, when they went to the warehouse together. She could have told him then. People said things then, when they were close. It was possible that she'd talked about him, and his daughter. The thoughts began to blur and run, panic came down on him.

His hands trembled, he was crying. Not loud, not sobbing, but just the constant flood of tears that always happened when he was upset – all part of his illness they had told him.

When he heard the swish of tyres, saw the headlights, heard the door, his gut clenched, his heart thundered, he leaned over and puked into the water; nothing but bile.

This had been a stupid mistake, what had he been thinking?

He got up, began to run, slipping in the wet. There had been a time when he would have stopped, turned, confronted the bastard. He would have taken him on, broken his arms and legs if need be and then handed him in. Made him pay for the things that he'd done. There was a time when he was strong enough to do that. Not anymore.

Suzanne had been scared; terrified really. He'd recognised the look, had seen it on the faces of young squaddies, back in the day. She'd been brave though – misguided, and stupid, and crazy, but bloody ballsy. He'd told her to stop what she was doing, told her it was dangerous, but she never listened, she wanted what she wanted and that was the end of it.

For him to have done that to her, pretty Suzanne with the golden hair and the soft skin; for him to have reduced her to what he'd seen carried out of the warehouse – there'd been no need for that. Just another body bag, just like the others, too many others, in too many different places. The tears came faster, and it was hard to breathe.

He heard footsteps. His feet were sore. He couldn't go any further.

He stopped and looked around. It was darker now; the river was an oily ribbon at his side. The rain washed the tears from his cheeks. Bushes behind him rustled. He spun on his heel. The dizziness was on him again, he needed to breathe properly but his chest had tightened, there was no room for air. He couldn't remember when he last ate, the last time he had a drink. There had been no time. He'd had to move, had to dash to get here. It had taken it out of him. Not like in the old days, the route marches, proud and strong. This had turned him into a rat, scurrying along a run and now the bloke was here, and he was afraid. It made him scurry faster, gasping. He'd made a mistake; stupid, stupid. He was a fool.

"Meet me by the river, I'll bring the money." What a crock of shit.

He should have gone to the police, but they would have made him go inside, taken him into small rooms, asked him questions. There would have been court, people, lawyers and judges, questions and accusations, shouting and pointing. He felt sick at the thought of it.

There was a pain deep in his chest now and his fingers tingled, he needed oxygen, there wasn't enough in the world.

He shouldn't have come. He had wanted to make this scum pay for what he'd done to Suzanne. But now he saw, money wouldn't bring her back, nothing would bring her back. Leanne was better off without him anyway, and they'd agreed: no more contact.

He sank to the damp grass of the riverbank, wrapped his hands around his knees, closed his eyes and waited for the man. All he'd wanted was justice for Suzanne and some money for his little girl.

Chapter 37

"Bloody hell, you look awful." Charlie bent to take Tanya's bag and for once she didn't bother to argue or even be irritated by his old-fashioned manners.

The taxi that eventually picked her up, at the end of the road of huge houses where Fiona lived, had dropped her at the station with barely time to collect her ticket from the machine and scutter to the platform. She collapsed into the dusty seat, pushed her bag behind her legs, and her laptop case beside her against the wall. She wrapped the shoulder strap around her arm and, once her belongings were as safe as she could make them, leaned her head into the corner and let herself fall into a pit of sleep.

Charlie had driven the one and a half hours to meet her so that she didn't need to drag herself through the ups and downs of Birmingham's new station and stand on the draughty platform waiting for a connection. The sight of him, smiling broadly, outside the ticket barrier almost overcame the strength that had seen her through the ordeal with her sister. She was overtired, and it was making her emotional. He had a huge cup of takeaway coffee in his hand and she'd swapped it gladly for her bag.

"I probably look pretty much how I feel, to be honest," she said, holding up the coffee. "This'll see me right though. Thanks, Charlie."

She had thrown away the sling but had already given him an email account of what had happened.

"How's the arm?" he asked.

"Pretty sore to be honest. I took some pills, but the pain was there as soon as I woke up. It'll be fine but right now it's a bitch."

"Take another pill. You can sleep in the car."

Tanya shook her head. "No, they make me groggy. I need to go to the office, I need to get up to speed. You can fill me in on the way. I had some thoughts, watching that video. The witness. Oh, and have we found Colin the Cartman?"

Charlie held up his hand. "Okay, okay. Let's get in the car first. No, we haven't found Colin, still looking. Bob Scunthorpe knows you're back. I sent him a text. He's coming in later to have a word. I didn't call the team in; did you want me to?"

She had meant to tell him to do that. Now, groggy from the journey, and with an arm on fire, she was glad that she hadn't.

"Let's see how things go. Maybe later, or more probably first thing tomorrow. No point spoiling their weekend for no real purpose," she said.

Despite her early intentions, the warmth of the car and the quiet thrum of the tyres on the motorway were soporific, and Charlie let her sleep. She woke again when they were quarter of an hour from headquarters and it was easiest to sit quietly, gather her thoughts and wait until they were in the office and she was back, in charge and home.

Chapter 38

As they walked the corridor leading to their shared office, Tanya breathed in the familiar smells. A hint of cleaning products, dusty carpet, and humanity. The pale walls, grey industrial grade floor covering, and the chipped woodwork welcomed her, and she smiled.

Throwing her bag in the corner, she booted up her laptop and plugged it into the peripherals. Charlie switched on the kettle and soon the smell of instant coffee joined the fug. She leaned back in her chair and closed her eyes. It was over, she had done her duty – more than her duty, taking into account the throbbing in her arm – and now she could move on. The sense of freedom didn't last long.

"How were things with your sister?"

Charlie's question brought her back to earth with a bump. Of course, it wasn't over, you couldn't cut the past out of your life and not expect a scar. She looked at him for a moment screwing up her face and then gave him a quick precis of the morning's conversation. He looked upset on her behalf. Charlie with his ever-expanding Jamaican family – new babies nearly every year among the various couples – didn't understand, and obviously didn't believe, that what she wanted more than anything was to have nothing more to do with her sister. He didn't argue but he shook his head sadly.

She moved on. "Right, I want that bloke back in, Freddy Stone. I want to interview him myself. I watched the interview with Paul and Dan and there was just something."

"What something?"

"Well, first of all, he'd just left a pub; there'd be a toilet there. Why didn't he go in comfort?"

"Well, you don't always, do you?"

"No, and it's probably nothing but it struck me as odd. Mainly though it was about who he saw. He was very vague, we've jumped on the idea of the homeless guy, but I want him to tell me in more detail. I didn't trust him."

"Hmm." Charlie turned away, sat behind his desk and began to fiddle with the mouse and keyboard.

"What, what's the matter?"

"Nothing, it's just that, well, you know, the team."

"What about them? I already said I might get them in later."

"No, that's not what I meant. We've been working our butts off on this. There's hardly anything to go on and..." He paused.

"Spit it out, Charlie."

"Well, I reckon that if you start re-doing all they've done it might get their backs up a bit. It's been disheartening, to be honest, not moving forward that much and this business–" He waved a hand between them. "They had trouble knowing who was running the show. If they get the idea you're going to re-do everything... well, I just think that maybe you should be a bit careful how you handle things."

"Sod that."

"Right." With the one word he left the office and she could hear him moving about in the incident room.

Tanya closed her eyes and rubbed a hand across her face. Dealing with people wasn't one of her strong points but she had made headway with this team. In large part it was because of the way Charlie had handled her taking over the last case and now she had annoyed and upset him. She lowered her head to the desk muttered into the wooden top, "Why the hell does it always have to be so bloody hard?"

There was no answer.

Chapter 39

Tanya pointed at the screen. "Look, there. When Dan asked him who he saw in the alley, he doesn't answer right away. And when he does reply, it's vague. 'Probably just that homeless bloke.' Why would he say that? And note he said, 'that homeless bloke'. How does he know there's a homeless bloke if all he did was go in for a pee? Does he go in there regularly? It's just as if he is saying what he thinks we want to hear somehow."

Tanya had run the video again in the incident room. Though he had said very little, Charlie had no choice but to watch it with her.

"So, why are we looking for Colin the Cartman?" she asked.

"The beat coppers said that he was the most likely rough sleeper. It's one of his favourite spots. Plus, he's disappeared since the fire."

"Okay, all valid points I grant you but…" She turned to face him. "You do see what I'm getting at, Charlie? Maybe because I was away, maybe because I wasn't part of the sense of – oh, I don't know – wanting to move it on quickly." In spite of her earlier thoughts, she was treading carefully and didn't want to say 'desperation'. "Perhaps I looked at it more coldly."

"Yes, okay. I guess you've got a point. But this is going to go down like a lead balloon, you know that don't you? They're going to feel as though they missed something. It's given us something to concentrate on, it felt like a move in the right direction and now you're saying it's nothing," Charlie said.

"I'm not saying stop looking for him, it's all still viable. All I'm saying is let's get this bloke Stone in again and push him a bit. I didn't like him, he was shifty."

"Bloody hell, Tanya, more than half the people we have in here are shifty." Charlie gave a laugh, but it was devoid of humour. She knew that telling him it was just a feeling wouldn't cut any ice. All she could do was insist and try to minimise any antagonism.

Further conversation was cut short by the arrival of the detective chief inspector and while Charlie trailed off to the almost empty canteen to chew at a stale ham sandwich, Tanya related the events of her trip to Scotland.

"I'll put a call in to Stan Laird tomorrow," Bob Scunthorpe said. "Make sure we can preclude another trip up there, for the moment at least. I need you up to speed on this warehouse fire."

"Yes, sir. I've been kept up to date by Detective Inspector Lambert, and the team has been doing a great job." Maybe if she praised them with the seniors it would filter back and take some of the sting out of what she was doing. It didn't quite work.

"I haven't seen a great deal of that. A couple of interviews, a search for a rough sleeper but no progress," Scunthorpe said.

"We have identified the victim, sir."

"Yes, but it's told us very little, except that some poor streetwalker was where she shouldn't have been and paid with her life."

"Yes, sir." There was nothing else she could say, he was right.

"I'm going to do some interviews in the morning. I'm going back to the site. I'm on this, sir," Tanya said.

He nodded and flicked the cover closed on the thin file in front of him. "We have to find some justice for this young woman. It doesn't matter how she came to be in that situation she still deserves our best efforts."

"Yes, sir. I hope that you're not under the impression that we haven't been putting in our best effort. I'm sure the team has been giving it everything they have."

He looked up at her, "If this is the best effort then it hasn't been very productive up to now, has it? You know very well how important the early days are, how these cases become cold. I know you had to go to Scotland, that wasn't in doubt, but we need to make sure that hasn't compromised this investigation or we'll all have to explain ourselves and our decisions."

On her way to find Charlie, Tanya had to concede that he was right. Bob Scunthorpe was a fair and honest boss. She knew that when they looked at this later, her trip to Scotland, which he had sanctioned, could well be held up as a contributory factor if they didn't solve this murder. She had to break it open in the next day or two or it would get away from them and simmer in the background waiting for a stroke of luck maybe for months, even years. That wouldn't do her career any good at all, and the knock on would affect the team. All except for Kate Roberts and maybe Paul Harris, they were ambitious and yearning for promotion. Well, they were just going to have to get behind her, hurt feelings or not.

"Inspector Miller."

Tanya turned to see a uniformed constable hurrying behind her, a hand raised in a 'hold on' gesture.

"Yes."

"You've been looking for a rough sleeper?"

"Colin the Cartman."

"Right. Well, they've found him."

"Excellent." She had spun round and was heading back to the office, her phone already in her hand to call Charlie away from his solitary lunch.

"Well, not that excellent actually. He's dead."

Chapter 40

The atmosphere in the car was less friendly and relaxed than just over an hour before. Tanya spoke first: "I do take your point, Charlie. I can understand what it's been like and I appreciate all you've done. Especially as you could have been sitting on your arse watching daytime television."

He nodded and glanced at her. He gave her one of his grins, the sort that had Sue Rollinson lusting after him.

"This is more than likely going to change things, eh?" he said.

"Not many details as yet." Tanya clicked open her phone to read the report of the discovery. "A couple out for a bike ride along the riverbank found him. Ruined their jolly afternoon, I reckon. Mind you, who goes for a bike ride in this weather? Serves them right."

"He wasn't in the water though. Thank heavens. I hate drownings. How sure are we that this is Colin?"

"Pretty certain. Luck more than anything, and let's face it we should be due some by now. The mobile patrol that turned up when the 999 came in recognised him from when he was on the beat," Tanya said.

"Out near Shire Lake Ditch. That's quite a distance, if his usual place was round the warehouse."

"Yes, I wondered about that. We'll have to speak to some of the people who knew him."

Charlie didn't need to explain the groan. They both had experience of trying to elicit information from homeless people and rough sleepers. Apart from the surroundings they inhabited, they were naturally suspicious of authority.

"Yep. I know, but I want us to do it rather than farm it out to the uniforms." Tanya clicked off the phone and settled in the seat. Her arm throbbed constantly and she wished she'd hung on to the sling. She tucked her hand inside her jacket, pulling the zip up just far enough to give a bit of support.

"You okay?" Charlie asked.

"Yeah. I'm okay. I reckon we can just have a word with our cyclists, and Simon Hewitt when he arrives. The SOCO team have been scrambled and death has already been confirmed by the on-call doctor. Then we'll decide the best response."

Silence fell again except for the quiet robotic voice of the sat nav and the patter of water on the windscreen as it began to rain.

"Shit. No, not more rain." As she spoke Tanya leaned forward, scanning the grey sky. "Why couldn't it just wait another hour."

"If we're lucky the team will have a tent up already."

"Bloody hope so. Please stop raining, please stop." She gave a shrug. "It's not stopping, Charlie."

"Nope, don't think it is."

Charlie parked on the gravelled road. A couple of expensive bikes propped against a tree showed them where the cyclists who had found the body were sheltered.

There was a blue plastic tent, telling them just where the body lay, near to the edge of the bank. A police photographer was videoing the area, stopping now and then to take a still picture. A few uniformed officers hung around, sheltering under trees, looking despondent. The rain was heavier, and they all knew it would be a fair while before they could get into the dry.

The van from the morgue was parked further along and Simon Hewitt's car nuzzled up behind it. Tanya's stomach did a little flip as she thought about the last time she'd seen him and remembered Sue Rollinson's comments.

The complications in her life were piling up and she was going to have to get to grips with all of it. She clambered from the car, straightened her shoulders and walked as purposefully as possible given that every muscle was pleading desperately to climb into bed and lie down in the warm. She accepted a white paper suit, shoe covers and mask and with Charlie bringing up the rear they walked along the bank to make the acquaintance of Colin the Cartman.

Chapter 41

They stepped into the blue plastic shelter. Although there was still a little daylight, it was heavy and overcast. Floodlights had been deployed, a small generator humming in the grass. The greens and browns of the riverbank were stark and artificial looking in the harsh glare. Simon Hewitt glanced up from where he crouched beside the body. He turned off his dictating machine and took a few steps towards them. "Charlie. Tanya. Good to see you. I heard about your niece. Is that all sorted now?"

"Yes, thanks. All sorted."

"Run away, had she?" He shook his head. "Who'd be parent to a teenaged girl?"

"Well it wasn't that simple, but you're right, I wouldn't have that job at any price." She didn't want to talk about this now. Right now, she wanted to crouch where he had been, examining this poor dead man who was dressed in wet, filthy rags, his toes visible through holes in the worn-out trainers.

Simon Hewitt was obviously in the mood for a chat though, "Are you okay? You're very pale."

"I'm okay thanks, Simon. It's been a difficult couple of days." She took a small step to the side, crouched beside the body. "So, what have we got here? Poor bloke. Not had a lot of luck, has he?"

The medical examiner took the hint. He coughed and bent down beside her. "Right, yes. I believe we already have an identification?"

Tanya nodded.

"That was a stroke of luck. I have only just begun my examination and obviously I can't tell you very much until I have him back in the morgue, but he's probably late forties, maybe fifties. These people age quickly, a result of their circumstances obviously. He appears to be badly undernourished."

"Any idea what the cause of death might be? I know it's early days but any chance it was natural causes, do you think?" Tanya asked.

"Not unless a polythene bag over your head can be considered natural, no."

He held up an evidence bag. "Removed by the people who found him, there was no point really. Still, I suppose they meant well."

"What's that in the bottom?" Tanya asked.

"Glue. It's on his face as well."

"So, it could have been an accident? He could have been sniffing?"

"It's a scenario yes, but there are these." Simon Hewitt pointed to a line of red marks on Colin's throat.

"Are they fingermarks?"

"I would say so. He may have sniffed the glue voluntarily, but I believe somebody held the bag over his head. The glue could be an attempt to put us off the scent. Of course, they may have helped us, we'll get some information from those." He turned to one of the assistants moving carefully around the little space. "Bag his hands now, would you? We might get something, though the nails are bitten down to the quick. Still, you never know."

"I reckon, we'd better get things moving," Tanya said. She turned and walked out into the cold rain, pulled out her phone and dialled Bob Scunthorpe. She told him she was about to instruct the uniformed officers who were already there to start a local search, before the deluge had a chance to obliterate any more evidence. She asked for whatever extra help he could send. They agreed that the chances of this being a coincidence and not connected with Suzanne Roper were slight to none.

"You'd better get the team in. The sooner we get on with this the better," she said to Charlie.

"Are you sure?"

"What?" She glared at him as he spoke.

"No, I just mean you do look dead on your feet. If you like I could take this. I know the drill, I'm up to speed. You could get a lift home. Get some rest. Take your pills. You could start fresh in the morning," he said.

"I'm fine, Charlie. Thanks, but I'm good." She put her head back into the tent. "Thanks, Dr Hewitt. I'll attend the post-mortem."

"I'll get Moira to give you a ring. Tanya, take care you don't look well."

She smiled at him and nodded, he was only being friendly. She turned to find Charlie, his eyebrows raised grinning at her. "Bloody hell, what is it with you lot?" She pushed past him and stomped up the path to talk to the now soaking officers whose shoulders slumped even further as they realised that a fingertip search on the wet riverbank was the only thing in their immediate future.

"You know what to do and the sooner you get to it the better. This weather is not our friend. We are looking for anything at all. There will be evidence bags and marking tents in the SOCO van. Is everyone clear about how to do this?"

They nodded at her with varying degrees of enthusiasm.

"One thing, this man had a shopping trolley. All his worldly belongings were in there and it's not with him. I can't see him leaving it anywhere voluntarily so bear that in mind. It shouldn't be hard to find," Tanya said.

"Unless it's in there." One of the young constables pointed at the grey, rain-speckled water.

"Yes, there is that. We're going to need divers, Charlie. Could you get onto that?"

"I don't expect there'll be anything to find but we must look. Even though he hasn't actually been in the river as far as we can tell, who knows what might have been thrown in. If the trolley was in there you would have thought there'd be floating debris but yes, we need the underwater team," he said.

She glanced back and forth along the road. "Bloody hell, if there were any tyre tracks here they'll be mud pie by now. What a cock-up."

She climbed into the car and turned on her tablet computer. She might be tired and in pain but there was no way she was handing this over, not to Charlie, not to anyone. Colin the Cartman was hers and he was going to help her find who burned up the poor dead prostitute.

Chapter 42

After the round of 'welcome backs' and a couple of 'how
are yous?' said in the tone that meant 'you look terrible' the
team settled into what had become their usual places in the
incident room. Tanya perched on the edge of the desk
nearest to the noticeboards. She looked around at the
familiar faces and grinned.

She thanked them for what they'd been doing, told
them she was glad to be back. It felt like a waste of time,
mollycoddling grown-ups. But it was expected, and Charlie
had already shown her what could happen if she put their
backs up. She glanced at him. His face was unreadable, did
he know this was all because of him and his warnings?
Probably. She hated treading on eggshells and moved on
as quickly as she could. Once it was done she got down to
business. The death of Colin, and the brief preliminary
findings at the crime scene were discussed and then she
assigned tasks.

"Kate, phones and collating. Oh yes, and before I
forget, get in touch with that Freddy Stone bloke, I want
him back in. Tomorrow. Half ten in the morning – okay?"

She didn't expect a comment from Dan but was
surprised when Paul didn't defend their work. Maybe she'd

got it right after all or maybe it was simply this latest development had them focused on the case, instead of their fragile egos.

"The rest of us are going to find some of Colin's acquaintances."

Kate glanced out of the window at the rain, which was now very heavy, she grinned and nodded. "Yes, boss."

There was sighing from the others, Paul muttered under his breath about it 'bloody pissing down', but she had expected it and knew that it meant little. It was a matter of honour with blokes like Paul to moan a bit.

"It's a good time to catch them. We need to do the hostels. Dan, Paul, do it together, will you? Kate will you get them a list, and while you're doing that can you find out if there are any vans that go into the area, dishing up meals and drinks, that stuff. If there are we'll probably need help from the uniformed branch to cover all of it.

"You'd better make a start because we've got about three hours until they are all going to be bedded down, or out of their heads on cider, and we don't want to try and talk to them then.

"Charlie, Sue and I will make a start with the ones on the street. Okay? Anything you can get about his recent movements. We need to find out if he had said anything about the fire. He disappeared from his usual haunts – why? And, where was he? This could be a move forward and I don't want to waste the momentum. If anything pops up, let Kate know immediately. Kate keep us all informed." She looked at her watch. "It's half five now. Give it to half-past nine and then call it a day unless we have something. Back in tomorrow by seven. Everybody okay with that?"

"Do we have a picture of him, ma'am?" Dan asked.

"We don't yet. Kate, get on to the morgue? Ask them to send one to us as soon as possible. Something we can use to show around, so they'll need to clean the poor bugger up a bit first. When it comes in, zap it through to all our phones. In the meantime, they mostly know each other anyway, and it's not an identification enquiry. We know who he is. What we need now is to find out where he's been since Thursday and why." She glanced at the windows running with rain, turned back and grinned at them. "You might need your sou'westers. But look on the bright side, they'll all be taking cover."

Leaving behind a chorus of low-level grumbling, Tanya walked into the office and lowered herself to her seat. Her painkillers were in the pocket of the leather jacket drying on the chair back. She popped open the box and stared down at the blister pack. It was so tempting. Anything to dull the throbbing in her injured arm and the constant complaint from bruised and overtired muscles. It had been bliss on the train. She sighed and slipped them back into her pocket. She'd take them later, for now a coffee would have to do. She couldn't go out in the darkening streets, searching in shadowed corners and dingy alleyways with her wits dulled by drugs. She made the coffee strong and loaded up on sugar. It was a couple of hours that was all, she could do this.

Afterwards she was going home to take a long, long shower and slide into her own bed. The mental image crumbled as she realised that she hadn't spoken to Charlie about his accommodation. She couldn't face entertaining a guest. If he was still at her house, is that what it would be? She puffed out her cheeks, blew air through her lips. When did life become so bloody complicated? When Fiona rang, that was when. Not for the first time in her life she roundly cursed her sister. It helped – a bit.

Chapter 43

They took Charlie's car. Sue Rollinson's old banger, a hand-me-down from one of her brothers, was only a two-door and it was rusted and dented. Although it wouldn't look out of place where they were headed, it was not a good advert for the force.

Tanya slid into the passenger seat, throwing her handbag into the rear beside Sue. From experience she checked first for baby toys but there were none. She wondered how Charlie was coping with not seeing his son on a daily basis but she wasn't about to ask him personal questions with Sue sitting in the back seat. By the same token she wouldn't ask him about his overnight plans. Would it really be that bad if he was still sleeping in her spare room? The poor bloke only had a half empty, deserted house to go back to. He knew about her injury, her aches and pains. Probably he wouldn't expect her to play the hostess. She had enough to worry about without stressing over this. She pushed it aside. It would be what it was.

They parked in The Castle Multi-Storey. It was close to the last known sightings of Colin and near the storage units. Outside, the rain didn't show any signs of letting up.

Sue pulled up the hood on her jacket and Tanya had to make do with turning up her collar. It seemed that she was fated to be soaked, cold, and uncomfortable.

Charlie and Sue turned left towards the shopping centre and Tanya headed down the alley, past the site of the fire. The burned-out unit had been boarded up with sheets of chipboard. There was a 'Danger – Keep Out' notice nailed to the front. There was still crime scene tape at the entrances to the narrow road. She needed to get on to the fire officer and find out if it was safe for them to go in yet.

The area was deserted, and after a quarter of an hour finding nobody, she called the others back to the car. "Let's hope Dan and Paul have more luck at the hostels. This rain has sent everyone looking for shelter."

In the time since they left the car park, a small group had huddled, out of the rain, in a corner under the pedestrian footbridge.

The three of them were recognised as police as soon as they arrived at the car park entrance. Of the six men and one woman huddled against the stone wall, three got up and walked away.

Charlie took the lead, hands in his pockets, casual and non-threatening. "It's okay, guys. We just need to ask you a couple of questions."

The older man in the group hawked and spat onto the pavement. Tanya felt Sue Rollinson tense beside her.

Charlie was still speaking quietly to the three men. The woman sidled closer to one of the younger ones and placed a hand on his leg. They were suspicious and on edge but at least they weren't drunk or spaced out on drugs, though they were passing a bottle back and forth.

"We're trying to get some information about Colin the Cartman." Charlie waited, watching for any reaction. The four pairs of eyes stared up at him. "This one of his spots?"

The older one coughed again. "What's it to you?"

"We wondered if you'd seen him around in the last few days? The beat bobbies said he'd disappeared. After the fire." Charlie waved an arm in the direction of the entrance opposite.

"Disappeared. We're all disappeared," the old bloke muttered. "Only time you see us is if you're movin' us on or looking for drugs. What's he done anyway? Poor bloody sod."

Tanya leaned forward, looking the man in the eyes. "Why do you call him that?"

"What?"

"Why is he a poor sod?"

"Huh, why do you think?"

Wet, cold, hungry, dirty. Yes, it had been a stupid question. The man was speaking again, his voice a rough growl. "On top of everything else, poor bugger pushing that trolley around everywhere, collecting crap and carting it about. Pathetic."

Charlie leaned closer. "So, when did you see him last?" The only response was a shrug and another hawk and spit. They were going to have to go further if they stood any chance of getting them to say much more. They hadn't wanted to mention Colin's death. It was too much, too soon but it looked as though they wouldn't have a lot of choice. It was impossible to know how they might react, they could clam up completely, afraid that there was to be an investigation and they would be involved.

Sue stepped forward and held out a bag of toffees. The group in the corner just stared at her, until the woman reached out a grubby hand and thrust it into the bag. "Yeah, thanks. I like these."

"Here, have them. I've got another bag in the car." Sue handed the sweets over and moved closer to lean against the wall. "So. Colin. Do you know where he's been? Why he vanished?" she said.

The girl turned down the corners of her mouth. "Just wanted leaving alone, didn't he? He was gutted about what happened."

"Was someone not leaving him alone then?" Sue said.

The older man butted in, "Well you're not, are you? Harassing him. You should let him be. He didn't have anything to do with that fire. No matter what you think."

Tanya shook her head. "We haven't been harassing him. The patrol guys were keeping an eye out for him but that was all. We thought he might have seen something. We could hardly harass him when we couldn't find him, could we?"

"He was upset. The bloke's a bit fragile anyway and he was freaked out by it all. Anyway, we don't know where he is. And why don't you leave him alone? Spend your time looking for whoever started that fire. He said he couldn't trust you lot to do the job, not with the girl being what she was."

"When did he say that? I thought you didn't know where he was," Tanya said.

"I don't. This was straight after. He was rambling on about it, about the law and justice. He'd lost it a bit, she was a sort of friend to him, it shook him up. I reckon he used to be clever – before he went to pieces. Anyway, he wasn't impressed with you lot." The man had bent to pick up a backpack sitting on the damp pavement. The others shifted, and looked back and forth at each other – they were losing them.

"And none of you have any idea, yourselves?" Tanya said.

"About what?" The girl asked.

"About who started the fire?"

Without another word, the group rose from their damp seats, turned and walked away.

"Shit."

"Can't we take them in?" Sue said.

"What for?"

"Well, withholding information."

Tanya shook her head. "We don't know that they are. Anyway, it'd get us nowhere and it would antagonise them. Once we're ready to release the news about Colin we'll come back. If they hear what happened to him, we might have more luck. It's not a total bust. Sue, ring Kate, tell the lads to call it a night. I think we've got all we could have hoped for, to be honest. Come on, Charlie can drop you back to pick up your car."

She wouldn't ask him now, she would wait to see if he said anything about where he was staying. She didn't want to make him feel unwelcome in her home. Even though he was.

* * *

He watched them go, they were obviously police. The woman who had walked past the burned-out unit didn't need a uniform to declare her profession.

He could go after the group of street scum, offer them money, wine, a greasy meal from one of the disgusting cafes, find out what had been said but you couldn't trust these people. They operated in a different reality. They were like the whore, saying one thing and then doing something else. They didn't know anything, they couldn't. He had taken care of everything. But maybe it was time to move. Time to put his plans into action. Sooner than he had meant but no matter, it was all in place. A few loose ends and then he would go.

He turned away, pulled the collar of his long overcoat tighter around his throat and walked into the darkness.

Chapter 44

The house was warm and welcoming. Charlie insisted on carrying her bag from the car. He dumped it down beside three others already in the hall.

"I've nearly finished getting my stuff together. I meant to stick the sheets in the washing machine, but I didn't have time. I'll do that now if you like," he said.

Tanya felt the warm wrap around her. She thought about him turning out into the foul night, heading towards a cold, empty house. He was the nearest thing she had to a best friend. For God's sake, she probably wouldn't be here if it hadn't been for him fighting off a deranged killer intent on choking the life out of her.

"Stay if you like, Charlie. Why don't you just stay until this is over? It'll make things easier. You can do the driving, I reckon. It's tricky with this." She moved her arm gingerly.

"Are you sure? I mean, I know how you like your own space."

"Yeah. Mind you. I'm not cooking for you and stuff though."

He laughed. "No, but I could cook for you, I enjoy it. I'd be grateful Tanya; my place is sad and empty. I could pay you something."

For a moment she was tempted, extra money – he didn't have any idea how much she needed it. But she shook her head. "Don't be stupid. We'll go halves on the grub though, okay?"

"Brilliant. Look, why don't you go and get yourself sorted and I'll make us something to eat. I really do appreciate this."

She stood in the shower, the water – as hot as she could bear – beating on her tense and knotted shoulders. The dressing on her arm was stained with blood. They'd told her that it might leak if she did too much with it. Well, it looked as though they were right. They'd given her spare dressings and told her to try and keep it dry. Right now, keeping it dry wasn't an option as the steam billowed around her and the thunder of water in the cubicle drowned out all the niggles and worries clamouring for attention. So, there was someone in the kitchen, sorting through her cupboards, using her utensils. What the hell did it matter?

* * *

It was still dark when Tanya woke but she'd slept the sleep of the dead. After stuffing herself with Charlie's jerk chicken – his granny had taught him well – they had finished with a pretty hefty glass of whisky each. She had dragged herself up the stairs and fallen onto the mattress, pulling the duvet over her face and breathing in the smell of home. She couldn't remember what they had talked about, but it had been easy and quiet. This was going to be okay. It was only for a short while anyway and he was good to have around. Carol was a lucky woman.

It was just after six and she was first downstairs and started the coffee maker. There was bread in the box and she made toast. With her laptop on the kitchen table she reviewed again, for what seemed the hundredth time, all they had. It wasn't much.

Charlie was dressed and ready to go when he came into the kitchen and she was suddenly very aware of her dressing gown and slippers. "Grab some coffee, Charlie, I don't know what you want…" She stopped, she wasn't going to do that – he wasn't her guest. Anyway, he was already reaching in the fridge for a bowl of fruit and a yoghurt.

"We're missing something, Charlie. None of it hangs together. It's as if it's bits and pieces with no common denominator."

She'd jotted notes on a pad in front of her. "We've got a dead prostitute. A burned-out storage unit with two high-performance cars. A dead homeless guy. Basically, that's it. No reasons, no connections. There are no answers, just why this and why that. I think we need to go back to the very beginning. Let's find out more about Suzanne Roper – everything. We still need to find where she was living. Have we found any bank accounts for her? We need to know whether she was still on the game or if she'd maybe managed to move on. We need more. I want to speak to Alan Parker. Then there's Colin, why kill him? He had to have known something. Not much to go on, is it?"

"Kate is already on to the bank account search and we've had the guys on the ground interviewing Roper's friends. Nobody seems to know much except that she hadn't been on the same patch for quite a while," Charlie said.

"Great, we need to do that ourselves, I reckon. Let's start to bring some of them in."

"I'll get on to that now, before they all disappear. You know, Freddy Stone is the only connection with Colin, it was his comment that started us looking for him."

"That's true. He keeps getting more and more interesting. There's something fishy about him. We've got him to interview this morning. Sit in with me. Right, let's get on with it."

Chapter 45

The girls were not happy. When the patrols on the ground were instructed to pick up any of the streetwalkers that were still around, they only found a few stragglers: women who had worked all night and were waiting for pimps to collect them and take them home, or the few who hung around during the day on the off chance there was a man with time to kill and an itch that needed scratching.

Tanya had asked that they were treated well, as much as possible, given something to eat and held in interview suites rather than banged up in the cells. She didn't need a pile of hacked off prostitutes to prosecute on top of everything else. Dan, Kate, Sue, and Paul did the preliminary chats.

Eventually Kate called up to the office. "Ellie Clarke. In interview room three. Knew Suzanne a while ago. She hadn't heard about her death and was pretty cut up about it. I think it might be worth your while having a word, ma'am."

The woman was skinny, dressed in a short leather skirt and a tight jumper. She looked tired and angry.

"Have you had something to eat, Ellie?" Tanya asked. The woman nodded.

"Had a bacon bap."

"Do you want anything else, more tea or coffee?"

"Nah. I'm good. Just want to get off home."

"I know. You've had a caution, I think?"

"Yeah, yeah, done all that crap. You'd think there'd be better things for you to do. What with all this terrorism and stuff. Knife crime, bloody kids on scooters robbing people, and you pick on us."

"I'm sorry about that. We have no real choice, you are breaking the law. Mind you, we could make that go away. If we could say you came in just to help us out. Because you're right, we do have other things that we are trying to do. I'm trying to find out about Suzanne Roper. Detective Constable Lewis says you knew her?"

"You can do that, fix it about the caution?"

Tanya nodded. "I can. So, Suzanne, you knew her?"

"Well, only for a bit you know, and I hadn't seen her for ages. I didn't know she was dead though; I heard somebody was, but I never thought it could be her. Bit of a shocker. She didn't deserve that."

"No, nobody deserves that," Tanya said. "We're doing our best to find out what happened to her, but we need help." As the woman raised her eyebrows and pushed the chair away from the table, Tanya held up a hand. "It's okay. I'm not asking you to do anything you'd be uncomfortable with. I just need to know more about her life, more about where she'd been living, that sort of thing."

"I don't know. I know she used to live in a shared house with a couple of other girls, for a bit anyway, but I reckon they've all moved off. I don't know where she'd been lately. She was a bit of a snob in a way, thought she was a bit above the rest of us. She wasn't though, was she? Not really. Just a girl on the game. Still, I'm sorry she's the one who got killed."

"Did she have a pimp? We've been asking around and we heard she might have had someone."

"She was straightening out, I know she was trying hard," Ellie said.

"Yes, we'd heard that as well. It's a shame. Trying to sort herself out and then this happened. Anything at all you can tell us might help. Even if you think it's not important. We're a bit stuck here. If it had been you, wouldn't you want her to help us?" Tanya wondered if that had been a mistake, but Ellie Clark nodded her head slowly.

"I don't know much. Big Mikey Malone ran her for a while. When she started to sort herself out, you know. I don't know if she was with someone before that, she never told me. I met her after she'd been had up the first time. Anyway, you guys put him out the picture. Mikey."

"Nobody took over his girls?" Charlie asked.

"You're joking. Somebody shopped him for GBH, he'll get out in a few years and nobody wants him looking at them, he's bad news. Knows some nasty people. No – they were left to fend for themselves. She hung about for a bit, stopped turning out so often, and then she just faded away. Haven't seen her for ages."

"Did she have no particular friends?"

"Ha – it's not like some bloody film out there, you know. We're not all mates. I suppose I was the closest thing and it was only because we're both from up north."

"So, you've no idea where she lived recently?"

"No, I already said. You haven't got a clue, have you? She's dead and you haven't any idea who did it. Poor bitch. Burned up I heard, and you lot, you're just flapping about like blue-arsed flies."

Bracelets jangled as Ellie bent to pick up her huge tote bag. She pointed a scarlet nail at Tanya. "You promised to fix this for me. Don't forget, yeah?"

With a disgusted glance in their direction, she strode out leaving the door to slam shut behind her. It was depressing to acknowledge that she was right. They still didn't have a clue.

Back in the incident room, they wrote the new names on the noticeboard. "Kate, can you find out about this Malone bloke?" Tanya glanced at her watch. "Charlie and me are seeing Freddy Stone in about ten minutes and then we'll have a conference this afternoon, four o'clock. I'm not sure what we've got since yesterday but we need to have a session. In the meantime, Sue, can you get on to Moira and find out what time they are going to post-mortem Colin? Paul, Dan get back out on the streets, see if we can find out any more about where Colin was and why he'd run. Was he running because of guilt or because of fear or, well, I don't know, something else entirely?

"Otherwise get your bloody thinking caps on people. We need to come up with something to move this on. Go over everything we've got so far and try and find me some bloody links. Charlie, we're still looking for Colin's trolley, can you make sure the street patrols are aware?"

She glanced at her watch. "You should be able to catch the briefing before they start their patrol. Kate, go through the reports from the search at the river, see if there's anything there I should know about. I should think if his stuff had been in the water we would have heard by now."

Tanya went into her office, read through the overnight reports and saw that someone had pencilled in an appointment with the detective chief inspector in the afternoon. She lifted the receiver to call his secretary and try to put it off for a while. She really needed to have something to tell him by the time she met him.

Chapter 46

Kate knocked once and pushed open the office door. "Have you got a minute, ma'am?"

Tanya glanced at her watch. "Charlie, can you ring down to the desk, ask them to show Freddy Stone into an interview room. Let him stew a bit. He's due in at ten. We'll go down there about half-past I reckon. Yes, come in, Kate, what have you got?"

Kate Lewis was carrying a couple of sheets of paper, she had a pen tucked behind her ear, tangled in her hair. She pulled at it and grimaced. "Shit. I really shouldn't do that. Habit. If you put a pen down at our house it's gone. Anyway..." She spread the papers in front of Tanya. "First off, Mickey Malone. Don't think that's going to tell us anything much. He's banged up in Long Lartin, causing trouble now and then. The word is that nobody will have anything to do with his 'girls' because of the repercussions when he comes out. Of course, it's impossible to know what's happening with his 'outside interests'. As far as they know he hasn't had a visit from Suzanne Roper, not under her own name anyway and if he'd phoned her, it must have been on an illegal mobile. Do you want to go and see him?"

166

"I don't think there's much point, is there? Not unless his name comes up again. I mean, if he left her to her own devices and she drifted away." Tanya shrugged. "Put that on the back burner for now. Is there anything else?"

"Yes, there is. Right. So, another thing I've been working on. The officers up in Leeds. The ones who went to break the news to our victim's aunt," Kate said.

Tanya nodded.

"I've printed out the report." Kate pointed to one of the papers. "Apparently she was less than devastated. Didn't want to know about her 'bloody niece'." Kate made quote marks in the air. "'Brought shame on the family. Running off to be a whore' and so on. Quite a rant. Anyway, she is refusing to have anything to do with claiming the body. 'Let them stick her in a pauper's grave like her poor mother' were the exact words I believe. She told them Suzanne had been asked to contribute to funeral costs and been unable or maybe unwilling. In the end, the council had arranged disposal of the body. Contact between the aunt and Suzanne had been by mobile phone, turned out to be a pay-as-you-go, long defunct now so that's no help.

"Anyway, I looked into it more. I contacted the local council. Of course, they were helpful because they thought maybe they could reclaim some funeral expenses. They have three years to claw it back, so they'd be pretty chuffed to find someone with some cash. I might have led them on a bit." She grinned. "Bloody local councils. Anyway, the mother died just over eighteen months ago. She wasn't married, divorced years ago, and the ex is dead. The aunt, only other living relative apart from the estranged daughter, is on benefits and disability. Broke, in other words. No insurance obviously. So, as we have seen, the body was cremated at a pauper's funeral.

"However, a while later someone paid for an entry in the book of remembrance and a memorial rose tree. It was done anonymously. This set the council's back up a bit as you can imagine, but when they tried to find the mystery person they drew a blank. They tried to trace the bank account, it was an online current account and by the time they got around to it, the account holder had closed it. Of course, the banks were a bit stroppy about giving out information. The woman I spoke to was a bit on her high horse about it all. However, she gave me what details they had, and I have a mate in the Financial Intelligence Unit, we do Zumba together."

"You do what?" Charlie said.

"Zumba, you know, the keep fit dance thing." Kate did a jiggle of her hips and grinned at him. "Anyway, the point is she did a bit of digging, they have more clout with the banks and it looks like it could very well be our victim. The address is a rental flat. I've been on to the agent, but they won't give out any much without a visit. They gave me the data protection spiel, but I'm on it. It's not that far away, I thought I'd get down there right now if that's okay, boss."

Tanya picked up the sheet of paper. "Oh yes, Kate, this is brilliant. At last a move in the right direction. Take Sue with you, get everything you can. They must have seen some ID. See if there's someone who remembers her. It looks like a breakthrough."

The other woman beamed back across the desk.

Chapter 47

Freddy Stone was irritated. He paced back and forth in the small room glaring at the constable who had been left to supervise. He spun around as Tanya and Charlie walked in.

"About bloody time. I was just about to leave. I don't know what's the matter with you people. I've answered your questions, I've told you all there is to tell you and yet..." He swept his hand in a half circle, taking in the room, the constable, all of it. "Here I am again, wasting my bloody time."

"Thank you very much for agreeing to see us again," Tanya said. "We won't keep you much longer." She was calm, quiet. It took the wind out of his sails. "Would you like to take a seat. Can we get you a cup of coffee, tea, water?"

"Christ sake. No. Look I just want to get off. What do you want to know?"

"I would like to go over a couple of points, please sit down. You don't mind if I record this, do you?"

"Do I have any bloody choice?" He threw himself onto the small plastic chair and propped his elbows on the table. "Get on with it then." His trainers drummed a tattoo on the floor tiles.

Tanya leaned over to look at his knee which juddered up and down. He shifted on the seat, leaned back with a muttered expletive, and folded his arms across his chest. Charlie set up the recording equipment. They went through the preliminaries; Freddy Stone mumbling his name in a sulky low voice.

"Mr Stone," Tanya began, "you have already told my colleagues that you turned into the alley off Crowell Road in order to relieve yourself. Is that correct?"

"Yes, no law against it." He snarled back.

"Well, there is actually, but we don't need to concern ourselves with that at the moment. You had been drinking in a local pub?" She was confident about what it was she was looking for. In the first moments after she had woken, Tanya had seen what it was that had been nibbling away at the back of her mind. She had a flashback to Edinburgh, the dark, wet night, Iain Laithwaite, waiting to meet his contact to collect more drugs, and then just before he walked back to the main road, having a pee in the entryway. Both things were a reason for a man to step into the darkness.

"Why didn't you use the gents in the pub? It's only around the corner, a few minutes away?"

Stone stared at her in silence, she saw a faint flush on his throat and bit back a smile. "I didn't think I needed to. Then I realised I'd... erm... made a misjudgement."

Tanya glanced at Charlie, he shook his head. "Not very nice though, out in the cold?"

"Look, I didn't know it was illegal. If that's your problem, just fine me or whatever. Christ, last time I try and help you people out."

Tanya ignored the outburst and picked up a sheet of paper from the file. "You said that you saw someone in the other end of the alley. Were you aware of smoke at that time, the smell of burning?"

170

"No, there was nothing. There was nothing when I was there. I hope you're not suggesting I had anything to do with that, are you? Anything to do with that fire?"

"Why would you think that?" Tanya said.

"Well, all this about me being there, dragging me down here again. I want a lawyer."

"Really?"

"Well, if you're suggesting I started that fire, yes. I heard somebody died."

"I didn't suggest you had anything to do with the fire. Did you hear me suggest that, Detective Inspector Lambert?"

"No, boss." Charlie hadn't needed to use the title, it was for show. Tanya smiled at him.

"Well, what is it about then?" Stone said.

She had unnerved him, all the cockiness had gone, he was defensive and nervous; his leg jiggled again. Tanya spoke quietly, "You said you saw someone in the alley?"

"Yes, the homeless guy."

"How do you know?"

"What?"

"How do you know it was a homeless man? You don't live in the area, we have your address here and it's quite some way away."

"Well, I just thought it was probably one of them. They are always knocking around there. The church there gives out free coffee, it attracts them."

"Did you see if he had anything with him?"

"What sort of thing?"

"A bag perhaps, something like that?"

"No, I didn't look that closely, I wasn't interested in him. He was just on his own, going off round the corner."

"So, you didn't score."

"What?"

"You didn't go into the alley to meet someone to buy some drugs? You didn't go further down, maybe as far as the warehouse? You didn't have an appointment with anyone?"

"No. Look that's enough. I don't want to answer any more of your questions. I've had it. This is entrapment or something."

"You're free to go at any time, Mr Stone."

"Right, I'm off. I'm not going to come in again, not without my solicitor."

"Thank you. We've noted that." As the door slammed behind him and Charlie made the commentary for the recording, Tanya shuffled the papers together and slid them back into the folder. "Hmm, that got him riled, didn't it?" she said.

Charlie nodded. "So, he didn't see Colin the Cartman, he made it up?"

"No, I think he saw someone. Maybe it was his dealer. Of course, he couldn't risk putting us onto them and presumably just remembered about Colin – that he was often in the alley – and saw it as a way out without incriminating himself. Hmm, it does make you wonder. Do you see him killing someone? Was he so worried that he chased Colin? I don't like him, not at all, but I don't know whether I see him as a killer. And that would open up the possibility that there are two murderers. I mean if he had been in the warehouse, the timings are off on the CCTV. So, was Colin in the warehouse?" She screwed up her face. "Hasn't helped all that much, has it? Why didn't Colin come to us? Why run?"

"So, we don't think Stone had anything to do with the fire?" Charlie said.

"Hmm, not sure. I don't think we should rule it out, to be honest. I see three possible explanations: he is innocent and was genuinely caught short, he was there to score, in which case what happened? Or, he was up to something else. Nobody else was seen on the CCTV; could be there's a lot he's not telling us and he's in this up to his skinny little neck."

Tanya glanced at her watch and gathered up her phone and bag.

"Anyway, I'm off to the morgue now, and then if Kate has got it sorted we need to go and look at what I hope will turn out to be Suzanne Roper's flat. I'm seeing the DCI later, hopefully I'll have some news for him by then."

They turned to leave. In the corridor Tanya handed the file to Charlie. "Could you have a word with uniform, see what drug dealers they know about in the area? And set up a meet with Alan Parker, will you? As soon as possible. I need to talk to him, I know you did the interview, but I'd like to meet him myself. It seems right."

Kate was waiting in the corridor, papers in her hand and a grin on her face. "Walk with me, Kate. I'm pressed for time. What have you got?"

"Susan Roper, tenancy. She has been there just over a year. They saw bank statements and set up a direct debit for rental payments. Apparently, they are supposed to have a photo ID for tenants, but I rather got the impression that if there's money up front they let some stuff slide. They saw utility bills from her last address. I guess that was the shared house. Anyway, she's paid the rent regularly and on the one check they did, the flat was clean and well kept, so they haven't bothered much since."

"Right, soon as this is done we'll get over there. You, me, and Charlie," Tanya said.

Chapter 48

Gowned and booted, Tanya joined the small group clustered beside the cutting table. Simon and his assistant, an obviously apprehensive student who was observing, and a photographer. Colin was already laid out with a cloth covering his genitals. He had been washed and was probably the cleanest he'd been in years. His long hair, still a bit matted, was pulled away from the grey face and bundled like a small dead animal at the top of his head. They had shaved his long beard and without the facial hair he looked younger, more vulnerable.

She hadn't attended a huge number of post-mortems, but they never bothered her. Once the examination started, Tanya would experience a sense of excitement as the chance of discovery filled her mind. It wasn't that she forgot it was a human corpse, just that she needed what it could tell her so that the death could make some sort of sense. A puzzle to be completed. She had never told anyone this, knew it made her seem hard and unfeeling. People expected something different, especially from a woman.

Simon stepped forward and paused for a moment. He closed his eyes briefly and gave a small nod. Tanya had seen him do this before. Today it moved her. They hadn't yet found out where Colin was from or how long he had slept on the streets. She could imagine that the last years, pushing his trolley full of junk, he had been harassed, ridiculed or avoided. Now, when it was all too late, Dr Hewitt was paying him respect. She was surprised to feel the swell of tears in the back of her eyes and blinked them away. This was not the time to start becoming soppy.

The post-mortem examination confirmed what they had all known to be true. Undernourished, scarred by various old wounds, and dead from suffocation. Simon switched off the recording and raised his eyes to look at Tanya.

"I'll be putting this in my report but, just so that you know, he didn't die from sniffing the glue, and there is no evidence at all of long-term substance abuse. He may have had a difficult and somewhat unhealthy existence, but he wasn't a drug user and certainly not a huffer. There is no rash around his nose and mouth, no specific damage to his heart and the damage to his lungs is, I would say, from long-term tobacco smoking, not inhalant abuse."

He continued his work and once Colin had been sliced and dissected, his organs removed and retained in preserving fluid, they left the assistant to replace what they could and sew him back together.

He would be kept for a while in the quiet chill of his drawer, the tag on his toe bearing just his given name and a number. If indeed that was the name chosen for him when he was born. They would try and trace someone to claim him, someone to mourn him, but the chances were slim.

Back in the morgue office, Tanya refused a cup of coffee but took a moment to chat with Simon under the watchful eye of his assistant. There was no mention of a drink away from work. No flirtation. It had all been a flight of fancy by Sue Rollinson and Tanya felt a hint of disappointment. She didn't want a relationship, didn't need that complication in her life, but it would have been nice to think someone looked at her that way. Sue was right, Simon Hewitt was pretty tasty. Tall, good-looking, dark brown hair and grey eyes with just the beginnings of laughter lines fanning out from the corners. She wouldn't mind being seen out with him, if she went out that is, and if she went out with anyone, which she didn't.

She picked up her bag, held out her hand. "Thanks so much, Dr Hewitt."

"Please. Simon. I thought we'd agreed." He smiled at her. *Yes, pretty tasty.* She felt a warm flush begin to creep up her neck. *Stop it, you idiot.*

"So, someone held the bag over his head then." It was a bloody obvious thing to say, and it was on the verge of gabbling to fill the quiet.

"Oh yes, the marks on his neck are pretty conclusive. The blisters on his feet were interesting, weren't they?"

"Yes, he spent his days walking the streets and now he gets blisters on his heels. I reckon he suddenly decided to walk further and faster than he had for a long time. Where from though? And was the place we found him his destination or was he just getting away? That's what I need to find out now."

"Good luck, Tanya. I hope you can find some family, it would be nice to see him have a proper send-off."

They both knew it was unlikely. Tanya left the morgue to where a pool car and driver was waiting for her, feeling depressed and unable to decide how much of it was because of Colin and how much because she had hoped vaguely that there had been something behind the silly idea that Simon Hewitt fancied her.

Chapter 49

By the time she was driven into the car park, Kate Lewis and Charlie were outside waiting. It had begun to rain again: cold September drizzle; and the sky was grey and heavy looking. They huddled in the meagre cover of the entrance.

"Where is everyone?" Tanya asked.

"Sue and Dan are back out trying to find people who knew Colin. Just in case. Paul is in the office collating what we've got so far, including the search at the river. They've come up with nothing much yet, by the way, and he's complaining about it. Said he thought Kate was supposed to do all that, thought it wasn't his job," Charlie reported.

"Did he? Well, maybe I should put him right. Anyway, Kate, let's go over what you got from the agent."

"Yes, ma'am. I have copies of bank statements that are the same account as the one from my Zumba mate. A tenancy agreement in the name of Suzanne Roper. As we suspected, they cut some corners it has to be said. No photo ID but apparently she had enough to pay the deposit, plus a month's rent in advance. She showed them three month's statements and the bank account is healthy, so they went with it. Nobody in that office remembers talking to her, they think it must have been weekend staff. So they couldn't confirm anything from the picture, which is a bit of a bugger for them if the owners get upset about police all over the property. I have to say they were looking a bit sick when I left. Did my heart good, it did."

It was already after three o'clock and Tanya had an appointment with Bob Scunthorpe in less than an hour. It wasn't going to work. She hated doing it but told them to go without her.

"We don't have a warrant so let's just see what we can find out. Speak to the neighbours. The main thing is to make sure it's not some other bloody Suzanne. I'll mention it to the DCI now and see if we can gain access tonight, assuming it's hers. Though…" She glanced at her watch again. "It's getting late. Look, let's just get on with it and I'll do what I can at this end. If this is her home, then we need to be in there. Keep me informed."

Of course they couldn't. She would have to turn her phone off while she was in her meeting and as soon as they disappeared into the gloomy distance she wished she'd made them wait. They could have done. It was seeing them standing in the inadequate shelter, rain dripping onto Charlie's shoulder that had made her send them off. Her judgement was slipping, her arm was throbbing again. She felt irritable and dissatisfied.

She refused a seat and the offer of coffee in the DCI's office, hoping that he would pick up that she would much rather get back to investigating the case, than talk about it. As soon as it was possible she asked him about the search warrant for the flat. But there was little he could do right then. They needed definite proof of the tenancy before they could make their request. She struggled to hold her impatience in check, how could she get that standing in his office with her phone turned off?

She filled him in with the report from the post-mortem, her plans to visit Alan Parker again and that she wanted another go at Freddy Stone.

"Do you think he's a person of interest?" the detective chief inspector asked.

"There's something off about his story, but there's nothing concrete right now."

They both knew they were achieving very little with the meeting and Tanya was dismissed with a promise that as soon as she had enough proof the flat belonged to their victim, he would get her a warrant.

Tanya stormed down the corridor to the incident room. She pushed open the door, yelled for Paul to follow her and launched herself at the stairs, speaking back at him as he ran to catch up. "We're using your car, I can't drive with this bloody arm."

"Yes, ma'am. Where are we off to?"

"DI Lambert and Kate Lewis are looking at a flat, could be Roper's. We're going to join them and we're going to have a good old root around. We're going to find something to link the victim to the warehouse, and the alley and, please God, Freddy Stone. And we're going to move this thing on before it gets stuck any further, okay?"

"Yes, ma'am."

Tanya stopped outside the door. "Right you go and bring your car, hurry up."

As her sergeant ran through the puddles, soaking his suit pants, water sploshing into his shoes, she stood under the portico and dialled Charlie's number. She grinned as she heard Paul cursing the rain, the puddles and 'the pigging, bloody British weather.'

Chapter 50

"What have you got for me, Charlie?" As she clambered into the car, struggling with the seat belt, bag, phone and the restricted movement of her injured arm, Tanya was taken aback as Paul Harris leaned over her, grabbed the buckle and clicked it into the housing. She looked at him, her eyes wide, and stopped mid-sentence. He blushed to the roots of his hair.

"Sorry, sorry, ma'am. I do it for the wife, she's always on the bloody phone and forgets. Shit, sorry."

Tanya was at a loss, it hadn't annoyed so much as shocked her. The sight of the normally blokey detective sergeant flustered and embarrassed was hilarious. But he'd been out of line. Of course, it had been a momentary lapse. She could just let it go. But this was Paul Harris, famous for 'laddish' behaviour. If she let it go, then would this grow to become something other than it had been. Surely not. *Shit, what next.*

"We'll talk about this later. Just drive out of this bloody car park, will you?" she said.

"Yes, ma'am – sorry."

Tanya shook her head. "Right, Charlie can you repeat that?"

"Neighbours have confirmed that the image we've shown them looks like the tenant of this flat. We've had no response to Kate hammering on the door, and believe me, when Kate hammers on a door you know about it." She heard them both laughing.

"Right. We're on our way, I'll get back to the DCI, ask him to move on with the warrant. With what we've got from the agents and now this, we should be okay."

* * *

The apartment was in a decent area in North Oxford, near to Cutteslowe Park. There was a cluster of similar blocks and newish houses in the surrounding roads, all well-kept. Although Tanya loved her house in the older part of the city, she reckoned that this would not have been a bad place to live. According to Kate the rent was quite a bit over a thousand pounds a month for a furnished two bedroomed place. They stood outside in the rain staring up at the small balcony where a pot of marigolds and petunias were just starting to look past their best.

Tanya had used the journey time to contact the detective chief inspector who was organising the search warrant. Paul Harris had driven in silence and joined the others in a subdued mood. Charlie frowned at him and glanced at Tanya who shook her head, mouthed 'later' but couldn't resist a grin.

"Kate, get on to the agents. Get someone out here with a key. With a bit of luck, the warrant'll be approved by the time they arrive."

The manager of the agency huffed and fussed and complained about the time, but when Kate suggested they may have to break down the door if they didn't have a key, she found a way to make it work.

Waiting for the warrant was frustrating, and there wasn't much they could usefully do until permission to enter was approved. They had a word with the immediate neighbours who told them that the woman living on the same landing was quiet, kept herself to herself, and didn't have many visitors. All useless and bland.

It was raining heavily by the time they walked back outside, and they ended up sitting in Charlie's car, steaming up the windows, sharing a bag of mints and going over things that they all knew already.

Within twenty minutes they had got hold of a key. The young agent who had turned up, officious and self-important, wanted to hang around, obviously looking for a story to tell his wine bar mates. Tanya took the little bunch of keys with their cardboard tag, signed the receipt on his tablet computer, and sent him on his way. He was disgruntled and disappointed. He might have argued longer but the rain was coming down in sheets now, dripping from the trees, running along the gutters. The occasional car swooshed past and just a couple of people, hunched and hurrying, dashed from cars and into the warm and dry.

Charlie and Kate were out of the car before Tanya had a chance to answer the call as it came in from Bob Scunthorpe. Paul Harris, who had been in the front passenger seat, barely speaking, clambered out behind them. She could put him out of his misery, tell him it was okay and not to worry, but she was enjoying his discomfort. She could report him, send him on a sensitivity course; in truth he probably needed that. She had already decided she wasn't taking it any further, but it would do him good to worry for a while longer. Maybe it'd make sure he was on her side if she ever needed it. Cynical perhaps but you did what you had to do. He trudged through the puddles after the others, through the narrow hallway and up to the second floor.

Chapter 51

Though it wasn't very large, the flat was bright and airy. They opened the door, Tanya yelling out that it was the police and they were entering the premises, but they already knew it was empty. It had the closed and silent feel of a deserted property. They stopped in the hall to pull on blue nitrile gloves and to cover their damp shoes with plastic protectors. As they moved down the hallway, Charlie and Kate turned into the bedroom and Paul went into the lounge. It was tidy and clean, but the kitchen stank of a rubbish bin badly in need of emptying.

Tanya walked across the tiles, batting away flies the nearer she came to the sink unit. Obviously, the bin was inside the cupboard and when she opened it the smell was intense. The lid lifted automatically, and she peered inside. She didn't expect to find anything too dreadful, but it was still a relief to see only empty food containers and what looked like decaying fish skin, which was the source of most of the stench.

There were a couple of glasses on the draining board, a pair of rubber washing up gloves and a dishcloth folded over the top of the tap. It was all very ordinary, and very tidy.

Tanya left the kitchen and joined the others in the bedroom. They had begun a preliminary search of the drawers and cupboards, but they would need to bring in the SOCO team to do the job properly. The wardrobe held jeans and skirts and jackets, a few dresses, all on hangers, some of them covered with plastic bags. They were divided into colours and weights, winter and summer. Belts were hung on hooks behind the door. Shoes were bundled in the bottom, high heeled court shoes, trainers, flats. Tanya glanced at the drawers the others were examining, everything was folded, even the knickers, bras and scarves were in organisers, neatly tucked into their separate spaces.

"Bloody hell, she was a neat freak. I should take pictures to show my girls," Kate said.

Tanya turned back to the wardrobe and the mess of shoes. "Charlie, give me a hand with this, will you?"

They lifted out the footwear and she felt around the edges of the wooden boards. They knew already what this was all about, it was just a question of finding the way in. At the rear corner was a tag of black plastic. "Photographs, please, Charlie." He pulled out his smartphone and made sure the date and time stamp would be recorded on the images. It was a neatly made box, the sort of hiding place that would be useful for jewellery, or important papers. Or several bags of white powder, more containing colourful pills and blocks of dark resin. Tanya didn't touch them. She didn't need to.

"Send me the images, Charlie."

While they waited for the SOCO team to join them, they had a perfunctory look around the rest of the flat, but they knew they had found the mother lode. Tanya was impatient to get back to her incident room, so they could record all of this and decide where it took them.

"I want Freddy Stone back in. Tonight. Tomorrow first thing, Charlie, we need to move things along with the hunt for Colin's shopping trolley." She allowed herself a smile.

"This is big, this is what we've been looking for, we just have to find out who was involved with what. Right, back to headquarters. Charlie, you wait here until the SOCO team arrive, Kate and I will go with Paul if he can promise to keep his hands to himself."

The final comment had the detective sergeant blushing yet again and the others looking from one to the other in total confusion. She spun on her heels and marched out of the flat grinning broadly.

Chapter 52

"Right, let's get on this." Tanya stormed into the incident room leaving Kate and Paul scurrying to keep up. She brought the rest of her team up to date, including the four civilian assistants who were helping to collate the paperwork and watch endless CCTV footage, looking for Colin's last walk.

"These drugs," she passed her phone to Sue to look at and pass around, "we have to assume that they play a big part in what has happened to this woman. It's impossible that they don't. So, how, why and who? Let's go back over what we've got. I want Freddy Stone in here now, he was in that alley for more than just a leak, I'm convinced of it. Either he was just in there to score, and it looks now that it could very likely have been from Suzanne Roper – why else would they both be there at the same time? – or, he was supplying her with drugs. Dan, take Paul and bring him here. We're not going home until we find the link in this. I'll clear the overtime."

"What about Colin, boss?" Kate asked.

"I don't know yet. Either he was involved, unlikely but not impossible, or he somehow found himself in the wrong place at the wrong time. Seems a bit extreme to chase him and kill him but he's dead and somebody did it."

"If anything occurs to any of you, go through Kate, she's got the best handle on all of it. I'm in my office, I need to ring the DCI and let him know what's going on."

Bob Scunthorpe was pleased but cautious. "It's a move in the right direction, I won't deny that. Drug supply and murder are not the same thing though, Detective Inspector, and why was she in the storage unit if she was meeting Freddy Stone? You've a bit to sort out yet. Well done though, keep on it."

She made a cup of coffee and took a couple of the painkillers, the nagging ache in her arm was coming between her and clear thinking. She would have a Red Bull if she needed it. Okay, she was messing with her brain, but there would be time enough to recover when all this was over.

It wasn't very long before Kate knocked on the door, sheets of paper in her hands. "I've got a couple of things here. I didn't know about them until I started to go through the things that…" She stopped.

"Yes. Until…"

"Well, they were done while I was out. A fair bit has come in from the lab."

"Who received them?" Tanya asked.

"Erm…"

"Detective Sergeant Harris?" Tanya didn't need a response, then she softened. "Kate, there was a bit of a thing in the car." She laughed at the look on the woman's face. "No, nothing really bad. He forgot himself for a moment." She told Kate about the incident with the seat belt and they had a laugh and then she sobered.

"So, we'll give him the benefit of the doubt. We'll assume that he was knocked off balance so much that he forgot to fill me in on what had come in. But I want a word as soon as he comes back," Tanya said.

"Yes, boss. Anyway, the lab has been able to get a DNA sample from the vomit."

"What vomit?"

"There was vomit in the door frame, probably protected from the heat by the door itself?"

"Do we have an identification. Colin, Suzanne, Freddy?"

Kate shook her head. "None of them I'm afraid."

"What? That can't be possible."

"Sorry, ma'am, but it's here. There's a report about Suzanne, she ate fish as her last meal and from what we saw in the flat, well, it doesn't seem that she was sick."

They paused for a moment thinking of the stinking bin, the evidence of the woman eating in her neat kitchen with no idea that within hours she would be dead.

"Okay, let's just think this through. Could it be that this vomit is from another time? People vomit in alleyways near to pubs, it's what they do."

Kate was already shaking her head.

"Apparently it was possible to match it to a stain on the floor that would indicate that the pool was inside, dried out by the heat, except for this small amount."

"Oh bugger, you know what this means?" Tanya said. "Somebody else was there. Oh Christ, just when it was all coming together." She threw her pen across the table. "Never mind, let's just carry on for now. Have you got anything else?"

"Still working through the stuff the civilians have been doing, but I thought you'd want to know about this."

"Yes, thanks, Kate. Let me know when the lads get back, will you?" She waited for the door to close before lowering her head into her hands and cursing with most of the swear words she knew and just a few that she made up on the way.

Chapter 53

Tanya heard Paul and Dan in the corridor and went out to meet them. Charlie was back, just turning into the incident room and he hung about to listen. "Where have you put Stone?"

"Nowhere, boss."

"How do you mean?"

"We haven't found him. Not at home, we spoke to his mum. He still lives with her. Nice lady, worried because he hasn't been back since last night. He hadn't turned up for his job, he does a shift in a bar and he should have been in by four. They said that he was usually pretty reliable," Charlie said.

He saw Tanya's raised eyebrows. "Yes, surprised us as well, but they seemed to think quite highly of him, to be honest. Just goes to show you. Anyway, we spoke to his best mate who also works in the bar and he hasn't seen him. Tried to phone him, no answer. He doesn't have voicemail apparently, so it just rang out for a while and then they gave up."

"Shit! He's done a runner," Tanya said.

Kate was already heading for the phone on her desk.

"Charlie, I'll arrange an alert for the ports and airports. You get on to traffic, get them watching for his car. We don't know how long he's been gone but we've got to look. Bugger it. I don't believe this. Will somebody organise a trace on his phone? Kate, you do that."

"Yes, boss, on it."

She heard the flurry as the rest of the team were brought up to date.

"Ma'am, could I speak to you?"

"Not right now, Sergeant Harris, I need to move on this." She assumed Kate had sent him, and he was standing with his tail between his legs, expecting a dressing down about the seat belt incident and his tardiness in reporting the DNA result. But he was holding up another piece of paper, waving it back and forth. She frowned at him and pointed at the visitor's chair beside her desk. He sat and waited in uncomfortable silence while she made her call, set the search in motion. She turned to him. "What do you want, Paul?"

"It's this report, ma'am. It's only just come in, it was on my computer. It had been sent to traffic by mistake and they have only just found out where it was meant to go," he said.

"Well, come on then, spit it out. What the hell is it? And if it's got nothing to do with Freddy Stone, it'd better be important."

"It's the cars, ma'am. The ones in the warehouse."

"Yes, what about them?"

"There were two. One was a Ferrari," he glanced at the printout, "the other was a Honda. Well, the Honda was stolen. The fire officer rang with the VIN. But the numpty who took the call assumed it was for traffic and just sent it on to them by internal mail. They found the theft report, but didn't know what it was all about, so it's been ping-ponged back and forth until eventually someone connected the dots."

"Right. Owner's details." She held out a hand. "I want to speak to them as soon as possible, and Alan Parker. I need to speak to him tonight. I want Kate in here right now. Come on man, move."

He was out of the door before she had finished speaking.

"Ma'am." Kate was at the office door in seconds, the whole place was alive, it was the first time they'd been so motivated.

"Kate. How do we know where Alan Parker was when his place went up in smoke?"

"His wife told us he was in Dubai."

"Did we follow it up? Do we have his flight details, copy of his ticket, anything from the border force telling us when he came back into the country?"

"I don't know, boss. I don't think so."

"Find out for me. Matter of urgency. I'd have known all this if I hadn't been buggering about in Edinburgh." She caught the look on Kate's face, and knew that she'd offended her with the inference that they'd let something slide without her there.

She began to pace the incident room; the air was sharp with tension. She marched over to Paul Harris's desk and glowered at him as he tried several times to call the owner of the stolen car. He replaced the receiver and shook his head.

"There's no answer, ma'am. I've left a message," he said.

"Where are they?"

"Harrogate."

"Right get on to the local nick up there, I want someone round to the house. I want chapter and verse. Exactly where it was stolen, time, location, everything and then I want CCTV of the area. I want to see who nicked that bloody car and how it came to be a part of my crime scene. Nobody will have bothered, you know as well as I do that it will have gone onto the database, been issued

191

with a crime number for the insurance and that will have been it. But we need to see who nicked it. Well, do it now, Sergeant, what are you waiting for? Come on man, move."

She felt the silence around her and knew that, if he wanted to, Harris could cause trouble for her. She had given him a dressing down in front of his colleagues. It was unacceptable. She turned away and stamped back into her office; she was upsetting them all. Right at that moment she didn't care. When the shit hit the fan it could cover her, just as long as, before that happened, she had found some sort of justice for Suzanne Roper, and even more now, for Colin, who she deep down believed was more than likely an innocent bystander in all of this.

Her mobile phone rang, she picked it up and stared at the screen. Fiona's name and caller ID, and a cartoon picture of the Loch Ness Monster had popped up. She clicked the off button. *'Not now. No, not right now.'*

Chapter 54

Three hours had passed, everyone was jaded and tired but there was no forward movement. Tanya let the civilians go, there was little more that they could do. Paul couldn't reach the owners of the stolen Honda, and the Yorkshire police weren't much help. It was late, the shifts that were on duty in Harrogate were dealing with speeding drivers and town centre drunks. 'First thing in the morning', was the best that Paul could get from them. It wasn't life and death, it was an old case, just a stolen car, and Tanya had to bite back her frustration.

"Did you tell them where it was found?" she snapped.

"Yes, boss, but they've no spare bods and the CCTV will take time to trace. Sorry, boss, there's nothing we can do."

She spun away and stood for a minute in front of the images of her victims. Kate held up the copies of Suzanne's bank statements. She had already gone through them with one of the civilians and they had highlighted interesting items. "Ma'am, do you want to see these?"

Tanya nodded, at least it was something.

The monthly rental payments for the flat were paid by direct debit. There were utilities payments and Boden,

M&S, Burberry and Selfridges were just a few of the names that poked at Tanya's conscience. Names she had become so familiar with. Suzanne Roper had been as extravagant and generous to herself as Tanya had been before the guillotine had come down on her spending.

Roper's accounts, however, showed no problem with the outgoings. There was a regular trickle which she had deposited herself, in cash at different bank branches. The amounts varied from a few hundred to a couple of thousand and other amounts were taken out in cash, again at different branches. There was no discernible pattern until April. A payment of nine thousand pounds had boosted the already healthy balance in the most active current account; it was moved within days to savings. It was just below the amount which would be cause for a money laundering alert. That alone was interesting, but there was another of the same amount the next month and another two months later, all shifted to a higher interest scheme.

"We need more information about those payments. Get on to the bank first thing in the morning, find out where they came from." Tanya told Kate. "She doesn't have a job, no family; the money she has paid in herself is more than likely the profit from her drugs dealing, all cash – we can't trace that. But this is something else and we need to know what. It looks as though she was building up a little nest egg. What with? What was she up to? Prostitution doesn't pay this sort of money and the drugs she had weren't in this league."

There was still no news of Freddy Stone. The street patrols were on the lookout near his home, a squad car was driving past regularly. Tanya would have liked someone parked outside but with a shortage of troops on the ground and lack of anything absolute about his involvement, she couldn't make it happen. She had to admit that it was highly unlikely he'd be wandering around at this time of night in the town, when he hadn't been home or to work. No, she was sure that he'd run, and it was going to be pure luck if they found him.

The mobile unit sent to pick up Alan Parker came back empty-handed. The house was in darkness, there were no cars in the drive. A neighbour taking her Labradoodle for its bedtime walk told them that she thought Mrs Parker had gone back to her mother's. She'd seen the car being loaded with suitcases the day before when 'little Benjie' had his morning walk.

"I shouted to her, 'off back to Cornwall then, Julie?' and she waved and smiled. Her mother's very ill, not got long I believe, so Julie goes down there whenever she can," the neighbour said.

They confirmed this by phone with an angry Julie Parker, furious that her ailing mother had been woken by the telephone ringing. She told them she was puzzled that her husband wasn't at home, but wanted to know just what business it was of the police anyway. "He's a businessman; his job takes him away from home and we don't live in each other's pockets so how the hell am I supposed to know?" she snarled before she slammed the phone down.

Tanya flopped into her chair. Blew out a huge sigh. "Bloody hell, Charlie, every way we turn there's a blockage."

"I don't think we're going to get anywhere now. Look, you've got the alerts out for Freddy Stone and that's the main thing. The rest of it will wait. I mean this stolen car, it might not mean much anyway. Okay, it makes Alan Parker a bit suspect, but we can look at it fresh tomorrow. Why not call it a day? To be honest, I'm not surprised; it's a funny sort of a job, I think."

"Yeah. You're right. We're going round in circles. Send the team home, back in at seven in the morning."

Chapter 55

Charlie and Tanya were in their office long before the shift change at seven. Neither of them had slept well and the night-time quiet of the building eased them into the day and their first cup of coffee.

Kate was the first of the team to arrive. She'd spent hours at home trawling through the bank statements again. She had spreadsheets and lists with highlights and sub-headings that made Tanya's head spin. Unfortunately, all it had done was to confirm what they already knew.

"I looked for other patterns, boss, but it's all so random. She was okay for money, more than okay to be honest. We probably know the source was drug dealing but I can't find any way for us to get to her supplier, or her dealers. She's been clever. I did wonder if she had more accounts and I've got my mate on that. Soon as the banks open I'm getting on to them about these big lumps though."

"Thanks, Kate." Tanya paused. "Kate, have you never thought of taking your sergeant's exam? You're so bloody good at this stuff, and you're a good detective anyway."

"No, ma'am. I'm fine, thanks. I'm happy doing just what I'm doing. I don't want any more responsibility and I need to have the time for the family."

"Well, I'm sorry we're cutting into that at the moment," Tanya said.

"Oh yeah, but that's always going to happen. I accept that, but as for anything else, I'm fine. But, hey, thanks for the vote of confidence."

"I mean it. If you ever change your mind, I'll back you all the way."

"Nah, too old." And with a grin, Kate went back to her desk. Tanya tried to imagine being so contented with what seemed to her to be underachievement, but it just wasn't possible.

When Paul flung open the door to her office a few minutes later, she knew immediately that something had happened. He hadn't even taken off his waterproof jacket. Drips of moisture ran from his soaking hair onto his forehead and he swiped them aside as he spoke, loud and animated.

"We've found Colin's shopping trolley, ma'am."

It was a small thing in the overall puzzle but seemed like a piece of good luck.

"Brilliant. Where? How?"

"One of the woodentops. Mate of mine, he has a bit of a connection with some of the rough sleepers. Apparently, it's hidden in a squat near to Colin's usual stomping ground. They haven't been in. Well, going into one of those places in the middle of the night, it throws up all manner of problems. But Steve the Squatter approached them. He'd been up in the north for the weekend, didn't know about Colin until last night. When he got back and heard about it he searched out Clive Pierce, to let him know."

"Right, I'm off down there. Charlie, can you hold the fort here?"

"He's in an interview room with a sausage and egg sandwich and a cup of tea, ma'am. When PC Pierce rang me, I asked them to bring him in."

"Okay." Tanya paused. "Where is the trolley?"

"Still at the squat. I've arranged for it to be picked up."

"Oh, right." Tanya was taken aback, it was unlike Paul to act without instruction. Maybe the bollocking in front of the team had done some good after all. "Thanks for that, erm, well done. I don't suppose there's much left in it now, mind you."

"Well, according to Steve it's been left alone. He took charge of it for Colin and he reckons nobody will have touched it when he told them not to."

"Seems a bit unlikely."

"Ha. You've haven't met Steve the Squatter, boss." And with a laugh, Paul turned back into the corridor, sliding out of his jacket and rubbing a hand through his wet hair.

"Well, that's intriguing. Where is he again?" Tanya called. Charlie had followed her into the corridor.

"Interview 3, boss. Do you want me to come?"

She knew he wanted to, in fairness he had brought this to her. It might help to mend the fences broken over the last couple of days. "Yes, with me, and well-done, Paul." She glanced at Charlie who nodded understanding and turned off into the incident room to join the rest of the team. The mood had lifted, they were energised again. It wasn't much, but it was better than yesterday's nothing.

Chapter 56

He was broad and muscular, with long legs tucked under the table; huge feet in scarred and dirty boots planted on the plastic tiles. The size of him alone would have been intimidating, but Tanya didn't think she had ever seen so many piercings and tattoos on one person. And she'd seen plenty. The plastic chair was almost invisible under the bulk of him and as Steve leaned forward across the tabletop, his bare arms were a mass of coiled snakes, daggers, anchors, bleeding hearts and names. Tanya tried not to stare but the pictures were mesmerising. When she looked up at his face he was smiling at her. A stud in his bottom lip shifted with the movement of his mouth. But his eyes were clear and the nod he gave her was friendly.

"Morning." His voice was quiet with the hint of a local accent.

Tanya held out her hand and as he shook it, he raised himself from the seat, just a little.

"Steve, is it okay if I call you Steve?"

He nodded.

"Detective Sergeant Harris tells me that you came forward with information regarding Colin's things. Thank you for that."

"No problem. I was really sorry to hear about him. Poor man."

"Can you tell me how the trolley... it is the trolley?"

Steve nodded.

"...how it came to be in your possession?"

"It wasn't in my possession. Colin asked if he could leave it at the squat for safe keeping. I told him I would keep an eye on it, and so I did. But it isn't mine."

"Ah, no, understood. So, did Colin tell you why he needed to leave it with you?"

"You have to understand that Colin wasn't always clear about his intentions. He had many problems and was often confused about things."

"Yes." Tanya nodded.

"He came to the squat late on Thursday night, upset and nervous. He stayed that night. On Friday morning he was incommunicative. Friday afternoon he went out for a while and when he came back he said that he would need to leave his things with me on Saturday because he had an appointment and couldn't take his stuff with him. Before you ask, he gave me no names, no locations."

"You didn't ask?" Tanya wasn't surprised when the answer was a shake of Steve's head.

"Wasn't my business," he said. "I just told him I'd watch his stuff. I warned him that I was going away on Saturday afternoon but I'm not sure that registered. It didn't matter, I told the others that they were to leave it alone. They left it alone."

Tanya believed him. He was calm, almost gentle but no one with any sense would annoy this mountain of a man. He didn't need to be anything but what he was. It was imposing enough.

"Is there anything you can add that might help us to find out who killed him?"

"Whoever it was must be a heartless bastard, excuse me, but Colin was a broken man. I see now that his upset on Thursday and Friday was because of what had happened to that girl. But I don't know why anyone would hurt Colin. But then, I don't know why people do the things they do. They confound me most of the time."

"Did you know the woman, Suzanne Roper?" Tanya asked.

"I did not. I haven't been around this part of town more than just a few months. I think she had moved away from the area before I arrived. I have heard talk since her death, not much more than reminiscences – people like to be the friend of someone in the limelight for some reason. But no, I didn't know her. I'm sorry." He unfolded himself from the inadequate chair and bent to collect his backpack. "I know I haven't been able to help you much, but I hope you find out who did these terrible things. I wish you luck."

He held out a hand and without a backwards glance, Steve the Squatter walked to the door. The uniform constable moved aside for him to leave. They heard the pound of his feet in the corridor as he went back to his chosen life.

Chapter 57

It hadn't told them much. They knew now where Colin had been on Thursday and Friday, they knew where he had ended up. They didn't know why. It had given them more frustration and unanswered questions, par for the course it seemed. When Tanya looked into the incident room to mark up the board and brief the team, Kate pushed back her chair and held up some printouts.

"Kate?"

"Boss, the large payments into Suzanne Roper's account. They came from the Middle East."

"What?"

"I know. I haven't been able to do anything since I had the news. It's still too early there. As soon as we hit their business hours, I'll get on to them. But, I have to say, my mate is doubtful we'll get anywhere. They will more than likely refuse to give us anything. We have no clout in that part of the world, nothing. Europe we'd be okay, even America we would stand a chance, but this is like Switzerland, maybe even worse."

"Okay. That's a bit of a swine. It does tell us more than we had before, but what? Unless of course she knew some Arabs. I wonder. Okay, stay with me on this. What if she had met up with some blokes from the Middle East in her line of work and they were paying her?" Tanya said.

Charlie butted in, "But why? I mean why bother. She could hardly blackmail them, could she? I think we're all thinking along the same lines, this has got to be blackmail, it has all the hallmarks. It's the only thing that makes any sense."

Tanya nodded.

"But if they were in the Arab world," Charlie continued, "why would they care? So, okay they came to England, used a prostitute. It's hardly shocking, is it? Who would care?"

Tanya sighed, "No, I suppose not, and anyway what has that to do with a scrappy little storage unit. Have we been able to trace that Alan Parker yet?"

"Sue's on that, ma'am. She's in the control room now. I'll check with her, but I don't think anything came in overnight," Kate said.

"Okay. I really need to speak to him, the bloody man. Tell you what, ring and find out if his wife is back from her mother's? We'll go over there if she is."

* * *

Julie Parker was back in Oxford, she did not want a visit from the police. She didn't know where her husband was and, even though Tanya was able to speak to her on the phone, she was unhelpful to the point of rudeness.

"Charlie, get your coat. I'm going over there. She says she doesn't know where he is. I don't buy it, she must have an idea. Bloody hell, it's her husband. There's the stolen car, and it was his warehouse that caught fire. He was in the Middle East when it happened, so there's a connection. There's no trace on the mobile number we have for him. It's bloody odd and she must know something. I'll see if I can arrange warrants to see his bank accounts in this country. It might not tell us much, but it will sure as hell piss him off. That'll teach him for messing me about."

At first Julia Parker refused to open the door. She screamed at them to go away. She was tired, she had just got back from her mother's house. Why the hell wouldn't they just leave her alone. This was nothing to do with her. But Tanya would not take no for an answer. She told her that if necessary they had enough evidence to apply for a search warrant. A car that had been in her husband's possession had been reported stolen.

The door opened slowly. The smart, together woman that they had met just a few days ago looked dishevelled and anxious.

She stood back to give them access.

"Are you okay, Mrs Parker?" Charlie said. "That's a nasty bruise on your face. Have you had an accident?"

She turned and walked back towards the kitchen and they had no option but to follow. She stood with her back to them. "Tea, coffee?"

"Thank you, tea would be good." It wasn't that they needed a drink, but Tanya saw that the woman needed time; needed to have something to do where she didn't have to look at them. Or them at her. She glanced at Charlie, raised her eyebrows and nodded her head out towards the hallway.

"Is it okay if I use your bathroom?" He didn't wait for a response but walked out of the kitchen and did a rapid search of the downstairs rooms. Ignoring the cloakroom in the hall, he ran upstairs and glanced into the bedrooms. He flushed the toilet. Without a warrant, they couldn't do more. There was no sign of Alan Parker, no sign of any other occupant.

Julie Parker carried the tray of mugs to the table, lowered herself to the kitchen chair and closed her eyes.

"Alright. Elephant in the room. Yes, Alan did this." She raised her hand to the yellowing, blue and red mark covering her cheek. "Yes, that's why I went to Cornwall. Though my mother is indeed poorly, and yes, he's done it before. I know all that you're going to say. I'm not stupid, so let me just tell you this. I am not going to leave him. I am not going to report him. I am not going to bring any charges. Take a look around you. I've worked bloody hard to acquire all this. My mum still lives in a council house in Truro. I'm not giving any of it up. Alan and I don't spend much time together. We hardly see each other and so, this," she stroked a hand over her face, "happens once in a while, that's all – when he's in a temper or he's stressed. This was because the insurance people were being difficult about the fire. For some reason he seemed to think it was my fault because I'd suggested the company to him. Anyway, it's done. I'm over it. So please, just leave me alone and let me get on with my life. Okay?"

"But you could report him. Take him to court. We could help you." Tanya had leaned towards the other woman, would have taken her hand if she had shown any inclination that it would be welcomed.

There was no humour in the laugh. "Ha! How would you do that? He knows where I work, he knows all my friends, my family, all the places I go to. Would you have me give up all of that? Hide somewhere so that he can't find me? Because he would find me. And if he found me, this," again she indicated her bruised cheeks, "this would be nothing."

"If you have any idea where he is, tell us. Truly, we can protect you. You can't just go on like this. Do you think he could have taken a car abroad?" Tanya said.

"I shouldn't think so. He doesn't take them, that would be ridiculous, they go all over the world. They are picked up in one place, mainly the UK and sometimes Europe, but then they are shipped in containers. On those big ugly ships. He has them in the warehouse, well he did until the fire. He does any tarting up that needs doing. When I met him he was just a mechanic, he knows his way around cars, I'll say that for him. Anyway, then they are put in containers and off they go, all wrapped in plastic." She shook her head and made a noise, it could have been a laugh.

She looked at Tanya, and laid a hand flat against her damaged face. "Oh, don't you worry, Detective Inspector, I live with this, I can. One day he'll get tired of it, move out himself, maybe go off with one of his whores. I can wait. Anyway, I really don't know where he is. He goes off, maybe collecting a vehicle, maybe meeting up with his horrible friends. As I've said we don't see much of each other. It's how I know that I can cope, until he buggers off one day and doesn't come back. It'll happen, I know it will. The sooner the better."

"Did you lie to us about where he was when the warehouse burned down?" Tanya asked. It had been instinctive. The woman was so very defensive, so keen to have them leave her alone.

Julie Parker just stared across the table for a moment, then she nodded and a moment later, shook her head. "It wasn't a total lie, he had been away, out to Dubai he'd told me, rubbing shoulders with other petrol heads, networking I suppose, in a way. He'd been due back on the Tuesday. He didn't arrive, I had a phone call from him to tell me that if anyone asked I was to say he wasn't back. I do as he says, it's easier. I don't know what he does, what he gets up to. I don't want to know, he mixes with people I don't want to have anything to do with. Dangerous people. If he says tell people he's away, I tell people he's away. I'm sorry."

She refused to let them call her a friend to stay, refused to report the abuse, see a solicitor or a counsellor. She just told them to go and leave her alone.

Back in the car Tanya had her tablet out, writing a rough precis of what they had learned. "Charlie, get on your phone, arrange an all-ports search for this swine, I want him found. I believed her, didn't you?"

"Yes, but what a bloody awful way to live," Charlie answered.

Once the calls were made they drove back to headquarters in silence, Tanya's mind was racing but not landing anywhere useful.

They gathered around the noticeboards.

"Anyone with any input speak up," Tanya said. "This has been staring us in the face. She told us he was away, we believed her. We didn't check, Christ we didn't check. Why not?"

Nobody had a response and they all knew that down the line there would be questions to answer and none of them would come out smelling of roses. Yes, Tanya would carry the can and to a lesser extent Charlie, who had been in nominal charge while she was away, but they had all missed it. What hurt most of all, and none of them verbalised it, was that maybe, just maybe, Colin the Cartman could have been saved if they had been more on the ball. It was a subdued gathering and a frustrating day that took them nowhere.

A report came in from Harrogate. The stolen Honda was seen once only, in the streets near to where it was taken, and then, if it was on the road, it had false plates thus wasn't picked up. They had no help to offer.

They went over it and over it, but it took them nowhere. They viewed CCTV from Birmingham airport, East Midlands, Liverpool, concentrating on flights to Dubai and the UAE. They called in passenger manifests from everywhere else. It made them feel as though they were doing something but knew that they weren't even scraping the surface of the possibilities. If they had missed him there was no way to bring him back from those countries and they all knew that they had probably missed him. Tanya managed to have a watch put on Parker's house. In the end, when they could go on no longer, chastened and depressed they trailed out of headquarters feeling like failures. Paul and Sue headed for the pub but none of the others had the heart for it.

Chapter 58

For a while they drove in silence and then Tanya rubbed a hand over her face and turned to Charlie. "Bloody hell, how did I miss this? Has it all been him?"

"We don't know yet. We can't know until we find him, and we can't do any more than we have done with that. You've got an all ports alert out. Traffic and foot patrols are aware, we've got his picture on the websites and Twitter. Tomorrow first thing it'll be on the news bulletins. Unless he's left the country already, we'll find him. And it wasn't just you, was it? None of us picked up on it. It's all so vague. Why? Was she blackmailing him because he'd used her services? I don't see that. I don't think his wife would care, she knew about that side of his life. It's not that he was in a job where it would matter. No, that doesn't gel. So, what did Roper know? We just have to wait until we find him. Then we can ask him, can't we?" Charlie said.

"If we find him. You said it yourself, Charlie. He could be gone already, and Charlie – where the hell is Freddy Stone?"

He had no answer for her but he knew she was thinking about the riverbank, and poor dead Colin. They walked into the warmth and comfort of her hallway.

"Whisky I reckon?" Tanya said.

Charlie nodded, went into the lounge to bring out the bottle. "Do you want anything to eat?"

"I don't think I can face anything right now. Let's have a drink, talk it though a bit, if you don't mind. You know, doing it at home."

"It's fine, it might help. Let me just call Carol."

"Okay, and I'll see what this is." She pointed at the answering machine, bleeping on the hall table.

It was Fiona, tearful and indecipherable. Rambling about Graham, Serena, misunderstandings, there was a sort of an apology lost in the confusion. She was drunk, there was no doubt. It was unsettling to hear her older sister in such a condition, but right then Tanya had no time or left-over sympathy. She put down the receiver and deleted the message.

* * *

They talked it through into the early hours and it all came back to Alan Parker and their monumental cock up.

"I'm going to have to go and see the DCI in the morning. I'll have to explain. I reckon he'll throw the book at me," Tanya said.

"No, no he won't." But even as he said it Charlie knew that there was going to be trouble. "Look we all missed it. We believed what we were told."

"Yes, but if I hadn't been haring off to Scotland we'd have been more organised."

"You're being overdramatic. Look, explain that we were lied to."

"Yeah, like that's going to help. We're lied to all the time, it goes with the job. It's our responsibility to check and we didn't. This is the end for me I reckon. Career's on the skids. I'm sorry, Charlie. I hope this doesn't screw things up for you."

"Tanya, you're blowing it out of proportion. You're done in. Take some of your painkillers, go to bed and tomorrow we'll deal with whatever comes, right?"

There was nothing else they could do.

* * *

She couldn't sleep. The calming effect of the painkillers had been overridden by pumping adrenaline and her brain wouldn't settle. She tried music, lying in bed with her earphones on so that she didn't disturb Charlie. She tried reading, but the words were meaningless shapes on the page. Every time she closed her eyes the re-run started again. She saw the charred and blackened body of Suzanne Roper, the burned-out cars and the pools of water lying on the floor. She saw Colin dead beside the river, his face smeared with glue, and the worn-out trainers which had rubbed up blisters on his filthy heels.

The thoughts jumbled with flashbacks from Scotland. With her emotions in turmoil she shed a few tears for her niece whose charmed life had been tarnished forever. She remembered that Fiona had rung but it was far too late to call her back, and anyway she still had to decide whether she wanted anything to do with that side of her life any more.

She slid out of bed and dragged her dressing gown over her shoulders. In the kitchen she had a drink of cold water. The garden was dripping. Moonlight shone on wet leaves and shimmered in puddles on the flagstones, but it had stopped raining. She watched the chase of silvered clouds for a while, tried to calm her racing thoughts, but then she was pacing again, between the kitchen and the living room.

Her arm throbbed, the stitches pulling as she moved it. That was something else that had to be sorted. She had to go and see the force doctor so that they could decide if she would need physio. She stretched and bent it, trying to convince herself that it was healing well enough on its own. She could flex all her fingers now without the shooting pain that she'd had just yesterday. She looked down at her hand. She could probably drive now. Her car was an automatic, she could clutch the wheel okay, surely.

Back on the landing she stopped and listened outside the spare bedroom. There was no sound, she whispered his name, "Charlie". He would tell her to wait until tomorrow anyway, and he'd be right, but this inactivity was torment and the house was closing in around her.

She didn't expect to find Freddy Stone, but maybe she could find the rough sleepers, have a word. Maybe she could talk to them about Colin, perhaps they'd remembered something. She put on her jeans and a thick sweatshirt, her leather jacket and boots.

It was easier than she had expected, driving the car. Not much pain at all and it was such a relief to be out, to be doing something. She reversed into the road and headed towards the car park in Crowell Road.

Chapter 59

The town was quiet, it was mid-week. One or two student types rolled home from some gathering or another but apart from that, the streets were deserted. The car park closed at 6:30 in the evening so Tanya pulled aside the crime scene tape and drove into the narrow road opposite.

The car splashed through puddles, jerking and jumping on the uneven surface. She tucked it in as close as possible to the boarded frontage of Alan Parker's storage unit.

She climbed from the car and left it with side lights reflecting on the wet pathway. She replaced the tape, it was unsafe and she didn't want injured pedestrians added to the mix.

There were no street lamps here, a couple of security lights gave some patchy illumination but the area around the fire site was in deep darkness and she considered turning her headlights back on. But she was out now, and she wouldn't be here long. She lifted the hatchback to fish out her torch and her can of PAVA spray, it was night in the city after all. It was cold, and the air felt damp.

Back at the main road there were no rough sleepers. The churchyard was dark and deserted and under the pedestrian bridge there were just a few empty lager cans and a fast food container. They'd been, and they'd gone. Wasn't that the way this whole bloody case had been? Chasing shadows and missing opportunities.

She glanced back and forth along the road, it was empty, and she was wasting her time. Instead of being at home sleeping so that she was ready for whatever tomorrow might bring, she was shivering in the cold wet outskirts of the city on a fool's errand with no real purpose. Her eyes filled with tears of frustration and she closed the lids and pressed her fingertips hard against them. She would not cry, not now and not tomorrow when she was sacked for incompetence.

She turned and walked back to the car. Coming nearer to the burned-out unit she could still detect the smell of scorched wood and charred plastic. She leaned a hand against the boards rattling them in the frame.

She almost missed the thud against the chipboard. She stood for a moment, listening. There was nothing more. She pushed against the boards again, banged on them with the side of her fist. She listened, there was nothing. Maybe it would be useful to go around the back and check that all was secure. She shone her torch down the alleyway. It was all potholes and puddles and she would have to walk to the end of the block before she could gain access to the backs. What would be the point?

There came another thud. Louder this time, beside her, against the chipboard. She stood side on and put her ear to the soaking surface. She thumped and waited, listening. There were two more thuds. She called out, "Hello, police. Is there someone in there?"

The response was another thud, a shuffling sound, another thud.

The boards had been nailed closely together to ensure a weatherproof seal and shining the powerful torch up and down the joins showed her no space where she could peer through. She ran back to the car and dragged out the heaviest thing she could find.

She banged again on the wood with the wheel wrench, the metal making dents and splinters where it connected. This time there was no response. She tried to find any small gap where there might be a chance to pry off the hoardings but with her weakened arm and the carpenter's excellent work it was impossible.

She could call for backup – get a crew down to break in. But then, if she was wrong, it would just be more fuel added the already smouldering failure of her handling of the case. It could have been anything, a strange echo, a reverberation in the wooden frame. What did she know about this stuff?

She ran down the alley, passed the fronts of the other units, stumbling on uneven ground, splashing through puddles and tripping on discarded cans and bottles. She turned left at the top corner, down the width of the last unit and into the deep blackness of the narrow walkway behind the block. She couldn't run now, it was too uneven and full of rubbish, but she slipped and staggered by the light of her torch until she came to the rear of the fire-damaged store.

She shone the torch onto the wired glass of the small rear window. It was blackened with soot and streaked with dirty water and she could see nothing.

She never heard the approach from the other end of the narrow path. She didn't see the glint of metal in the moonlight. It was a moment of pain and then everything went black.

Chapter 60

Nausea was the first sensation, followed by pain, followed by fear. Tanya opened her eyes to gloom and heard herself moan, before cutting off the sound as her senses returned. She turned to look around and felt the grate of grime against her head. The smell was awful, and it was this which told her where she was. It was the same stink that she had detected outside, but greater, stronger.

She moved her limbs and was surprised to find that she was free to push herself into a sitting position. Her eyes were growing accustomed to the meagre light. The nausea was abating, and she didn't think that she would puke. She swallowed hard, raised a hand to her head and felt the sticky residue of blood in a tangle of hair at the side. She hissed with the sharp pain of it as her fingers touched the injury.

There was no movement anywhere around her; it puzzled her. She curled her legs and raised to her knees. Dizziness held her for a while but eventually she was able to stand, leaning against the wall with one hand, and taking several deep breaths.

"Hello." As she called out she turned to peer around the unit. It was empty of the burned-out skeletons of the cars and the various bits of detritus that had been there before. That had all been taken away for forensic examination. In the rear she could make out the shape of scaffolding against the mezzanine. It had been put there to make it safe for access, she supposed. She took a couple of steps forward and that was when two sounds, almost simultaneous, stopped her. One was unmistakably a groan, which came from the corner nearest to the boarded-up frontage; the second was her car, she recognised it immediately. The rumble of the engine and then the sound of tyres splashing through the puddles outside as it was driven away. She panicked, fought against it and calmed herself.

Tanya moved towards the source of the groan: a dark shape slumped in the corner, curled into a ball on the filthy concrete floor.

Kneeling in the muck she reached out a hand, touched the head, moved her fingers downward to find the carotid pulse. Weak but regular. She leaned closer.

"Can you hear me?" There was no response. She shook the hunched shoulders carefully. "Hello, can you speak?" There was a groan and a little movement: the feet lifted and dropped, thudding against the temporary wooden wall, echoing the sound that she had heard outside – louder now at close quarters. Again, there was a groan, a mumble.

She bent closer.

"Freddy, is that you?"

The body tensed briefly.

"It's okay, Freddy, you're okay. I'm going to get us some help. You're going to be fine." She pushed her hand into the pocket of her jacket but of course the phone was gone. The can of PAVA spray was gone, the car keys were gone.

"It's okay, Freddy, we're getting out of here now." She sounded unconvincing to her own ears, but she heard him try to mumble a response. She ran her fingers through his hair but found no lumps, no sticky blood. "Are you hurt?"

There were no ropes or ties, no restrictions at all, so the only explanation that she could come up with for his condition was chemical. That was good. If he'd been drugged then even now he'd be moving towards consciousness, surely. She rolled him further onto his side and bent his leg and arm to support him, she tucked his hand under his face. Once she was sure he wasn't going to choke, she moved away and staggered to her feet.

By now her night vision made it possible to find her way around the space and she went to the small back door. It was closed – locked and immovable. She wasn't surprised, but she gave it a kick anyway. The shock screamed through her skull and brought back the dizziness.

"Stupid," she told herself.

Slowly she turned back to the scaffolding and, holding the cold metal bars, moved to the front where a ladder had been fixed alongside the burned wooden staircase. She rattled it back and forth. It was firm, and she gripped the sides and began to climb.

There was no logic to what she was doing, but her phone was gone, she believed her car was gone and there was nothing that she could find on the empty ground floor to help her. The office was the only hope of finding something, anything, that might break the glass in the rear window or hammer a hole in the wooden boards in the front.

Chapter 61

In the dim light upstairs Tanya could make out the shape of a desk, filing cabinets, and an office chair. It was still wet there and when she leaned on the chair seat she felt moisture squeeze from the cushion and dampen her jeans. The steel cabinets were cold but dry. When she tried to pull out one of the drawers the metal screeched like a banshee. "Shit!" She closed her eyes and waited for the pounding in her brain to ease. It must have been considered too dangerous to remove this equipment and there was, as yet, no sign that the SOCO team had been able to search up there. It made her wonder just how damaged the mezzanine was. She stamped a foot on the floor and felt it shudder under her weight, and heard debris falling into the room below. She should get back down the ladder.

There were papers scattered on the floor, it was too dark to make out what they were, but anyway they were creased, sodden, and disintegrating. There was no point trying to pick them up. She already had a good idea what had been going on there, and none of it would be written down on paper.

On top of the desk there was what at first she had taken as a box, but closer inspection showed to be a black, zippered bag. She lifted it, it was heavy, but it was dry. This had not been in the unit during the fire and the onslaught of the brigade hoses.

She pulled open the zip and tugged the top apart. She couldn't see what was inside so she dragged out one of the packages. There were many. There were other bags that rattled quietly as the pills inside were jangled together. This was like Suzanne's cache of drugs, it was just more of the same.

So, now she had confirmation – not that it had been needed – of the connection between Alan and Suzanne. More importantly, she had enough to arrest Alan, to look into all his dealings, find a connection between him and Colin, and then put him away for a long time. It would give Julie a chance to sort out her life. The thought was cheering.

All she had to do was get out from this locked unit before he came back for his bag. Plus, call an ambulance for the bloke downstairs, prove the connection between Suzanne, Alan Parker and Colin the Cartman – join all those dots – and all before they threw her out of a job. No problem.

She probably hadn't got long before he came back to deal with the loose ends, of which she was one, so she zipped the bag closed again, from habit more than anything, and climbed back down the ladder.

Freddy Stone was still lying in a heap but when she shook his shoulders he mumbled a response. She stood in the middle of the room, at a loss. Hammering on the wood would be a waste of time and energy, the area outside was deserted. She took off a boot and hammered against the window but the glass was reinforced with wire and shrugged off her assault with ease. So now, on top of everything else, she had a wet foot.

"What the hell are we going to do now, Freddy?" She knew he wouldn't answer but it reminded her that she was not quite alone.

Pounding at the glass had made her head and arm ache. It was throbbing again, and she felt her sleeve sticky where she knew it was bleeding. So, she'd buggered that up on top of everything else. Standing in the dark she was at a loss as to what to do next. Was sitting waiting for dawn the only answer? She felt pathetic.

Chapter 62

There came the rattle of the lock, the scrape of the edge of the door on debris, and Tanya scuttled back to the far wall, lay down in the grime and closed her eyes. The click of leather on concrete evidenced his passage, first to where Freddy Stone was possibly still in the recovery position. Would he notice? She held her breath, heard the shuffle of movement, a groan. She felt him come nearer to her, he poked her with his foot. The brightening of colour behind her lids told her that he had a torch and was shining it on her face. She mustn't react. Not yet. In her weakened state she wasn't sure that she could match him in a physical struggle. She had never met him, Charlie told her he was small, that didn't mean he wasn't strong. He had beaten Julie, he was a bully and he was probably worried and desperate. It made him a dangerous opponent. It was too great a risk with a damaged arm and a pounding head. He pushed roughly against her legs with the toe of his shoe.

"Hey, hey pig!"

Tanya concentrated on keeping her breathing low and even, her eyes closed, her face impassive. He kicked a little harder.

"Hey. Can you hear me?"

She sensed him draw back his foot, braced for the pain as he made ready to kick her harder. The scream of sirens in the road outside was salvation.

For a moment hope soared, she didn't know how it could be, but maybe help had arrived. Alan Parker cursed and ran to the rear of the unit, but the noise faded as the emergency vehicle sped past on the main road. She heard him laugh under his breath, then the clink of his shoes on the metal rungs of the ladder.

As he walked over the mezzanine floor there was the sound of broken ceiling cladding falling to the ground. The boards creaked and cracked with every movement. Tanya rolled over and crouched in the darkness, waiting, listening.

Freddy Stone spoke, "Oh shit. What the hell…"

The movement upstairs stilled.

It was time to do something. If he came back down, things could turn very nasty, very quickly. She rolled, clambered to her feet, leaning against the wall. Her injured arm screamed at her and there was another moment of dizziness. She pushed through them, turned and moved towards the ladder, planting her feet carefully, making as little noise as possible.

Freddy muttered again, "Hey, where are you? I can't see, man."

She willed him to be quiet, to not draw Alan Parker away from whatever it was he was doing. She climbed, instinct told her to hurry, sense told her to take care. Thirteen rungs. She swallowed hard as her head raised above the charred and crumbling edge of the platform.

Parker was kneeling in front of one of the cabinets, she heard the screech as he struggled with the drawer. She used the sudden, welcome noise to cover the quiet thud of her shoes on the final steps off the ladder.

His torch lay on the floor, the bag beside him. It was about four metres from where she stood. He had his back to her. She braced and stepped forward. Her foot kicked against the edge of a plastic box, invisible in the darkness. He was up and coming towards her before she had time to steady herself.

Tanya reached for the chair, dragged it in front of her. Alan Parker stopped, squinting through the dimness.

"Alan Parker I am arresting you on suspicion of the murder of Suzanne Roper..." She didn't get any further, he ran at her. She stepped away dragging the chair with her towards the rear wall.

He took a couple of steps, muttering under his breath. She swivelled the chair back and forth. Backed into the corner it was only a question of time before he dragged the chair from her weakened grip and then he would have her.

Freddy Stone called from the front of the unit, "Hey, man. What the hell is going on? That was some bad shit, man."

Parker turned his head towards the ladder. With all the strength she could muster, Tanya dragged the chair in towards her body and then launched it across the space. It hit his side and glanced off, toppling first onto the boards and then through the broken safety rail.

Alan Parker rocked on his feet, grabbed out at the upright at the top of the ruined staircase. Tanya ran at him, dived low and attempted to grab him around his ankles. He kicked out, his shoe connected with her jaw and, as lights flashed in her brain, just before the darkness came down she heard the splintering of wood, and his yell of horror.

She felt herself falling, heard the thunder as the upper floor collapsed and then there was nothing.

Chapter 63

Part of the roof collapsed as the mezzanine fell. The grey dimness of dawn lit the destruction: the tangle of blocks, wood, wires and roofing sheets. It was hard to breathe. Tanya's back was twisted, her legs were trapped, and the air was full of dust and soot. She coughed and tried to move – it was agony. There were a couple of pieces of debris across her thighs, but she was able to push them aside one-handed. Her arm was useless, just a mass of pain. Fractured she thought. Her mouth was swollen, she had bitten her tongue and broken a tooth. One eye was stuck closed with sticky mess that she supposed was blood. She wiped at it and pried it open to peer around blearily. She heard a groan and turned to see Alan Parker, a heavy concrete beam across his body. He was trying to push it away, but it was a hopeless task.

There was a trickle of blood from his mouth, bubbles of it as he breathed. She turned onto her knees and struggled across the mess towards him.

"Keep still, just stay still and I'll get some help. Where's Freddy?" she said.

She peered around but there was no sign of the other man.

Parker reached out his hand, clawing at her. She took it in hers and folded her fingers around it.

"I've got to get out, the wall has come down at the back, I can go and fetch help. But you need to keep still. Okay?"

He shook his head. "I'm sorry. Please help me. I'm sorry."

"I will. I'll go now."

"I didn't kill her."

"What?"

"I didn't kill Suzanne. You have to believe me. I didn't kill her. She fell. We were arguing, and she fell from the top of the stairs."

"But the fire?"

"I panicked. I panicked when I saw she was dead and... I'm sorry."

"Why were you arguing?"

He coughed and a spurt of blood splashed Tanya's face. He coughed again, and tried to push at the beam.

"She wanted more. All the time she wanted more. I'd helped her, taken her off the streets. I'd dealt her in. We had a good thing going, skimming off the top, just a bit from each shipment. But it wasn't enough – she always wanted more. Greedy bitch, blackmailing me, threatening to drop the customs people on me. I told her it would come back on her as well, but she just didn't care, all she wanted was more supplies. I couldn't do that, I gave her money and it was never enough. But I didn't mean to kill her. You have to believe me." He was crying now, the tears tracking cleaner lines across his face.

Tanya knew that she needed to get help, that he wouldn't survive without treatment, but he wouldn't let go of her hand and leaving him in such distress seemed heartless.

"I'm sorry about it all. Will you tell Julie, tell her I never meant to hurt her? I was on the edge, all the time. It was all a mistake. I should have stuck with the cars. That was fun, then I got greedy. I was scared, every day; scared that they'd decide I was no more use to them, or that they'd find out what we were doing. I should have told them no, right at the start but the money – it was so much money. I wanted to impress Julie with the money."

Tanya needed facts. She could see that he was fading, and this could be the last chance. Maybe it was cynical, but it was instinct. "What was it, what were you doing?"

"The cars, you can hide a lot of drugs in a car and I didn't think they'd notice the bit we were taking. When you do it regularly the customs people get to know you, they don't check once they know you. They just stamp the paperwork and wave you through. Keep clean for a long time and they know you. That's why I was useful, I was clean for such a long time."

"So, you weren't stealing cars, you or the men who worked for you?" she asked.

"No, no they were never supposed to steal cars, did they steal a car?" he looked puzzled for a moment. "No, that's wrong, they shouldn't have done that. It was one of the rules... never supposed to steal them and draw attention to them. Had to be squeaky clean, that's part of it.

"Me and Suzanne though, we'd got it sorted. Skimming just a bit, but enough to keep us going – just a sideline. Till she got too greedy, and we argued. I have to go away now, abroad, when I get out of here. I'll go away, I can't stay here where they can find me, not now it's all gone wrong." He coughed again; blood flooded across his chin and down on to his neck.

"Who are they? Who were you working for?"

He coughed out a sort of a laugh. "No, no. I'm not telling you that. How long do you think I'd last if I told you that?"

Tanya was struck by the poignancy of the question from a man who was so obviously on the brink of death. There were other things she needed to know.

"What about Colin?" Tanya asked. She leaned in, he'd closed his eyes. "What about the homeless man?"

"Collateral," Parker said, there was a rattle deep in his throat, a gasp, and she felt the grip on her hand relax.

"Alan, Alan. Can you hear me? Just hang on Alan, I'm going to get help." But she knew – even as she pushed to a crouch and struggled toward the break in the wall – she knew he was gone.

She staggered to the end of the alley, flagged down a passing car and used the driver's mobile phone to make the calls. Once it was done, as she felt herself sliding into oblivion, she managed to speak just one last time.

"Tell them there's another man. Underneath, they have to look for another man." Duty done, she let herself drift away.

Chapter 64

There was surgery on her arm, but apart from painful bruising and the damage to her face, which was all repairable, she had got away lightly. They kept her in hospital for four days. The DCI came to see her but wouldn't talk about her future. "Later, Tanya. When you're better. You did well, you solved two murders and, though we didn't bring him to justice, you caught Alan Parker."

"But the cock-up? My failure to check facts? What about that? I screwed up," she had insisted.

"There'll be an inquiry. It'll be looked at. Your personal situation will be taken into account, the business in Scotland. We'll have to wait and see what's decided. But first of all, you need to get well."

He smiled at her and continued, "On the upside, the drug squad is grateful to you. It seems that the people who sourced the cars for him were pretty well innocent, until they stole the Honda of course and that is very minor in the overall picture. But it has given them information they didn't have before, they have high hopes that it'll lead to more, quite a lot more.

"On top of that, it has highlighted some really serious failings by the customs and border forces. They probably have more reason to worry than you have, to be honest. I shouldn't be surprised if heads don't roll there. I expect most of it will be hushed up, of course. Well it's embarrassing, isn't it? You are going to be busy answering questions, I think you should be prepared for that. The whole thing will most likely roll on for a while and could become much bigger. I think you should be pleased."

It wasn't enough, and she worried about it constantly, sleepless in the uncomfortable hospital bed. There was nothing to do in the end but wait and hope.

When they said she was ready to be discharged, Charlie was waiting to take her home, but before she left the hospital Tanya went to see Freddy Stone.

Still attached to several machines, bandages on both arms and his face bruised and swollen, he had been much more badly hurt than she had when the mezzanine had collapsed. He had been underneath it, trying to reach the back door as the whole cascade of beams, concrete blocks, floorboards and furniture came down on top of him. It had taken them hours to dig him out.

"They won't give me long with you, Freddy, but please, just for my own peace of mind, will you clear up some things?"

He turned to look at her and tried to nod. "If I can," he whispered, "I owe you. If you hadn't brought help I would have died in that place under all that crap."

"We were both bloody lucky. You should know that as soon as they say you're well enough you'll have to make a full statement. I'm being forced to take sick leave for now, with all of this," she indicated her bandages, "and some other stuff, I don't know what's happening after that. So, just for me. Why were you there? Suzanne Roper was your supplier, yes?"

"Yes. I'd known her for a while, when she used to – well you know – when that was her patch. That was how we first started dealing."

Tanya nodded. "Right, did you know where she was getting the drugs?"

"Not at first, but then, a couple of times when I'd met her, waiting in the alley, I'd seen her going into that unit. I put two and two together, well it didn't need much to make it obvious. The night she died, I saw her going in there. I thought she'd be out in just a bit, so I waited. She was ages though and, in the end, I just gave up. I left her to it. I couldn't have done anything though, could I? I mean I couldn't have saved her?"

He paused for a minute, Tanya helped him take a drink from the glass at the side of his bed.

"I needed supply. I had people hassling me. I went back, hung around, found Parker. He agreed to sell me what I needed but the price was wrong. I told him I knew what he'd done. It was stupid but I told him. It was supposed to help me make a deal. Thought I could make some real money. I had people who were waiting for stuff, a good market. He agreed to deal me in. When I went to collect the first batch, he gave me some blow. A sample, he said. God knows what was in it, but it flattened me. I couldn't have saved Suzanne, I couldn't – could I?"

"I don't expect you could have," Tanya said. "Alan Parker told me that she fell."

"Why are you asking me about it though?" Freddy said. "Can't you ask him, he's the one that did it? And I think he was trying to kill me. He should be arrested for that."

"Alan Parker died, Freddy. His injuries were too severe and we're still trying to piece things together. With what he told me and the evidence we have, we're getting there. One thing though, why did you tell us you'd seen Colin?"

He looked at her blankly.

"The homeless man," she said.

"Oh, him. Is that his name?"

"It was."

"Yeah, was. Well, because he was there."

"In the alley?"

"Yes, I saw him, he was down at the end with that shopping trolley he always had. He used to follow Suzanne about, I think he had a bit of a thing for her. He was just standing there, and I thought that if you found him he'd say that he was in the alley and it would take the attention away from me. I didn't want to be blamed for the fire. I was scared shitless. I mean, a crazy, homeless guy – you'd look at him first, wouldn't you?"

Tanya watched as he shifted in the bed and a flash of pain moved across his face. He was quiet for a moment and then there was a hint of moisture in his eyes. He turned to look at her.

"Is it my fault he was killed? Is he dead because I told you he was there, and you went looking for him?" he asked.

"Well, you were suggesting he was to blame, pointing the finger to save your own skin. Anyway, we believe that Parker was responsible for Colin's murder. We got DNA from under the poor bloke's fingernails, it matched with some we got from the warehouse and of course from Parker himself so we know it's all linked together."

Tanya wondered for a moment if the kinder thing would be to say it might have happened anyway. However, that wouldn't be the truth, and in the end, it was truth that mattered.

"We don't know. The only people who can really answer that are dead, aren't they? We don't know why he met with Alan Parker or why Parker killed him, we can only guess. I'm sorry but it's something you are going to have to find your own peace with. As am I."

He nodded and cleared his throat. "I'm sorry. I know it doesn't make any difference, but I'm sorry. Am I going to be done? You know for the drugs?"

"Yes, you will have to answer for dealing drugs. You need to be prepared to be arrested, as soon as you're well enough."

"I suppose I'll lose my job."

"Yes, I imagine you will. There could be jail, but that's not for me to say."

Tanya gathered her things together and stood carefully, holding out a hand. He had a hard road ahead of him, he would carry some guilt for a long time. There was no need for her to hold a grudge. He nodded and touched one of his heavily bandaged hands to hers. "Get well soon, Detective Inspector."

"And you, Mr Stone."

Chapter 65

As DCI Scunthorpe had said, there was to be an inquiry. He tried to reassure her. "At the end of the day, Tanya, you were lied to deliberately. How much difference it actually made, it's difficult to judge."

"But Colin?"

Scunthorpe had shrugged. "We don't know that you would have found Alan Parker in time to save Mr Reece. That's something that they'll look at. I don't think you have much to worry about."

"The team… Charlie?"

"Again, we don't know that it would have made that much difference just knowing that he was already back from Dubai. His wife admits that she had no idea where he was. Okay, nobody picked up on it. It was an error, there's no denying it, but the chances of us having been able to trace him in time were slim. Tanya, try not to worry. Go home, rest, you still have some sick leave to take. I'll let you know what the feeling is if I can, and then I'll be there, at the inquiry. I've got your back."

* * *

They had searched through Colin's trolley. They found his surname, Reece, and his ex-wife's address. They had found medals awarded for his time in Afghanistan and his medical discharge papers, his sergeant's stripes, all wrapped together in his combat trousers. Muddy and dirty and sad.

He had a backlog of service pension that had been unpaid because he had no bank account and no address. Kate was in touch with his ex-wife who said that the money would be placed into an account for their daughter. She would be able to go to university if she wanted, her dad had made sure that her future was secure.

There was enough for a proper funeral, the whole team went, just so that there was a decent showing, but they needn't have worried. The British Legion did him proud and the United Kingdom Service Personnel and Veterans Agency made sure he had all the honours due to him. Some of the homeless people turned up. They sat at the back of the chapel, Steve was amongst them. They left as soon as the final music began to play.

His ex-wife came, alone. She sat at the front of the crematorium and laid a red rose on the flag-draped coffin. Later she sought out Tanya.

"Thank you, they told me that you did your best to find who killed him. He didn't deserve to go like that. But then, he didn't deserve to be abandoned to his PTSD, and he probably didn't deserve to be abandoned by me. But it was just too hard, after years of being apart so much, then his moods, his tempers, his depression. I couldn't cope. I let him down. We all let him down. Do you really have no idea what he was doing there, on that riverbank?"

"I'm sorry we can only guess. The man who knew is dead and he didn't have a chance to tell me." She would spare this woman the final word Alan Parker had uttered.

"I didn't bring Leanne. I'll bring her next week when this is over. She can bring some flowers, say goodbye. She's little and she has my husband as her daddy. But I won't let her forget him. He deserves that at least.

Chapter 66

Charlie went up north the day after the funeral. He would need to come back for the inquiry, but there was stuff for him to do with the new house in Liverpool and he couldn't wait to get back to Carol and Joshua.

They all had a meal together the night before he left. Charlie cooked, and the rest of the team came with flowers and wine and chocolates.

Tanya hadn't looked forward to the invasion of her home, but in the end it was okay. They didn't stay too late because she was still recovering. Sue, well-oiled with red wine, had cried a little too long and kissed Charlie a little too enthusiastically, but they'd laughed it off and put her into a taxi.

When they'd gone, and the kitchen had been tidied, Tanya and Charlie sat together in the candlelight.

"So, you'll get your house back tomorrow. You'll be glad to get rid of me," Charlie said.

"Oh, I don't know, it's been good having you doing the cooking. You're better at it than me."

"Well, thanks for letting me stay. You'll have to come and see us, up in Merseyside, when we're settled."

"Yeah. That'd be good. I think we've been here before, haven't we?" Tanya said. "You'd better make a run for it before anything else happens. I wish I could give you a lift to the station tomorrow, but they reckon it'll be another few weeks before I can drive."

"It's fine. Better to say goodbye here, I reckon. Then you can get on with your stuff."

She wasn't sure what stuff she would be getting on with. She wasn't allowed back into work yet, not even on light duties, but that wasn't his problem anyway.

As the Uber drew away the next evening, with Charlie giving a final wave out of the window, she turned and went back inside. It seemed quiet and empty knowing he wouldn't be coming back, but as the silence enveloped her, she smiled.

Her home, her space, her life.

Her battered leather jacket hung on a hook near the door. It was beyond hope, they'd cut the sleeve to remove it. Her wages were in the bank, she had her arranged overdraft and she really did need a new coat.

Tanya climbed up to the little office next to her bedroom and logged on. She wouldn't go mad. Just a jacket, maybe a new pair of boots. She had to replace the damaged stuff after all, and what was the point of the overdraft if she didn't use it?

While she waited for the computer to boot, she went back downstairs and poured a glass of wine. She was halfway up the stairs when the doorbell chimed. She frowned, glancing at her watch. It was after seven, at this time of night it could only be either Jehovah's Witnesses or sales. She climbed a couple more stairs, carefully juggling the glass in her injured hand. The bell rang again.

She sighed, stomped back down, and opened the door.

Serena stood on the doorstep, a huge backpack beside her. A taxi had parked beside the kerb, the driver standing near the open door.

"Aunty Tan." The girl was in tears. "Can you pay him? I haven't got enough cash and he won't take my card."

"Serena – what the hell?"

"Dad's gone, walked out and gone to live with his secretary. It's my fault. Mum won't talk to me. It's horrible at home. I can't stay there. It's hideous. I've come to live with you."

The End

List of characters

The Team:

Charlie Lambert – Detective Inspector

Charlie is tall and good looking. He is married to Carol. They have one baby who he dotes on. Carol is suffering from post-natal depression and Charlie struggles to support her and commit to his career. He is a family man from a large Jamaican family. Looking for his first high profile case as he climbs the professional ladder. Relocated to Liverpool after the 'angels' case. But held back to cover when Tanya goes to Scotland.

Robert (Bob) Scunthorpe – Detective Chief Inspector

Late fifties. Decent and honourable senior officer. Married. One son. Six feet tall with dark hair beginning to go grey. Supports the officers under his control, but is realistic about what is required of them to do the job and bring him results. Helped Tanya Miller in her early service with him.

Tanya Miller – Detective Inspector

Early thirties. Slim and fit, vain, shopaholic. Younger daughter in the family with one sibling. Always in the shadow of her brilliant older sister as they grew up. Now that both parents are dead she has all but lost touch with Fiona who lives in Scotland with three teenage daughters and a doctor husband. The results of always being an extra have made Tanya selfish and ambitious, always striving to prove herself.

Sue Rollinson – Detective Constable

Young, keen, hard worker. Unmarried, from a largish family, father dead, mother an estate agent.

Paul Harris – Detective Sergeant

A plodder. Recently married and a bit of a bloke. Doesn't really get the whole PC thing. Lives in a rental flat with his wife Nicole.

Kate Lewis – Detective Constable

Fifty, heading for retirement. Content with her life and achievements but refuses to be sidelined due to her age and lack of professional progression. Happily married with three teenage daughters. Accepting that she has stalled in her career. Skilled with the computer and a good organiser. Very fit, takes part in marathons and triathlons.

Dan Price – Detective Constable

Young and insecure. Quiet and keeps his head down. At just under six foot, with dark blonde hair and blue eyes, he is good looking. Lives at home with his parents and one kid sister who is still at school.

Simon Hewitt – medical examiner

Tall, good-looking, dark brown hair and grey eyes with just the beginnings of laughter lines fanning out from the corners.

Moira –mortuary receptionist

Late thirties and dedicated to 'protecting' the mortuary staff from hassle. Abrupt and unfriendly but tolerated by outsiders and affectionately so by the mortuary staff as she runs the place so efficiently.

Jonathan Bartlett – Senior Fire Officer

Bronze commander at the warehouse fire. Tall, in his forties, professional.

Tony Lyle – fire investigator

If you enjoyed this book, please let others know by leaving a quick review on Amazon. Also, if you spot anything untoward in the paperback, get in touch. We strive for the best quality and appreciate reader feedback.

editor@thebookfolks.com

www.thebookfolks.com

Other books by Diane Dickson

In this series:

BROKEN ANGEL (Book 1)
BRUTAL PURSUIT (Book 3)
BRAZEN ESCAPE (Book 4)
BLURRED LINES (Book 5)

The DI Jordan Carr Series:

BODY ON THE SHORE
BODY BY THE DOCKS
BODY OUT OF PLACE
BODY IN THE SQUAT
BODY IN THE CANAL

Others:

TWIST OF TRUTH
TANGLED TRUTH
BONE BABY
LEAVING GEORGE
WHO FOLLOWS
THE GRAVE
PICTURES OF YOU
LAYERS OF LIES
DEPTHS OF DECEPTION
YOU'RE DEAD
SINGLE TO EDINBURGH
HOPELESS

Printed in Great Britain
by Amazon